A NOVEL BY *ELIJAH NIGHTWELL*

SEALBREAKER

*He's trapped in his mind.. but what if
the demons are real?*

SealBreaker

© 2025 Elijah Nightwell

Published by Pennies Above LLC

ISBN: 979-8-9883106-9-3

Cover design by Joshua Pennifield

For permissions requests, contact:

joshuapennifield@gmail.com

Printed in the United States of America

Dedication

For the lost, wandering in silence, searching for forgiveness they fear may never come. May you discover that grace is nearer than the shadows that haunt you.

Table of Contents

Dedication 2

Table of Contents...3

Prologue...5

Chapter 1: The Celebration...8

Chapter 2: The Questioning Heart....................................18

Chapter 3: Circles and Signs 22

Chapter 4: Whispers in the Night.....................................28

Chapter 5: The Fraying Edge 33

Chapter 6: The Erosion..39

Chapter 7: Shattered Routine 45

Chapter 8: The Fractured Night 49

Chapter 9: Admission 55

    The Intervention...56

    The Departure..57

    The Hospital..59

    The Unit...61

    The Dream...62

Chapter 10: The Quiet Between Walls................................64

Chapter 11: The Thin Veil 70

Chapter 12: When the Walls Tremble.................................78

Chapter 13: The Breaking Point 89

Chapter 14: The Descent 95

Chapter 15: Clues and Allies..102

Chapter 16: The Forbidden Wing 113

Chapter 17: Night Terrors 126

Chapter 18: The Forbidden Pulse 136

Chapter 19: The Third Seal 144

Chapter 20: Shattered Alliances 155

Chapter 21: The Hollow Silence 161

Chapter 22: Into the Dark 170

Chapter 23: The White Room 183

Chapter 24: The Fifth Seal 193

Chapter 25: The Breach 204

Chapter 26: The Spiral 218

Chapter 27: The Sixth Seal 222

Chapter 28: The Seventh Seal 233

Epilogue 245

Meet the Author 249

Prologue

Rain pressed against the tall windows of Daniel Cross's office, the glass trembling with every roll of distant thunder. It was nearly three in the morning, but his desk lamp burned on, casting a pale circle across piles of books and loose-leaf papers. Whole towers of theology texts leaned precariously— Augustine, Luther, Bonhoeffer—and in the midst of them, a scattering of napkins, envelopes, and yellow legal pads, each marked with the same shape: a broken circle.

Daniel sat hunched forward, pen scratching with fevered insistence, as though writing faster might reveal the secret he'd missed in slower attempts. The clock on the wall ticked 3:07, but its hands seemed stuck, mocking him. His tie hung loose, shirt sleeves rolled back to the elbow, skin damp with sweat despite the cold draft from the window.

He muttered as he worked, words slurred into fragments. "Why her? Why us? Why me? What did I miss?" His voice cracked on me, so quiet it was swallowed by the storm.

Another page. Another circle. Another fracture drawn through it. The ink bled where his hand shook, but still he drew. His wastebasket overflowed with crumpled symbols, yet he couldn't stop. There had to be a pattern. There had to be an answer.

The thunder rolled again, deeper this time, more like footsteps pacing in the clouds than weather. Daniel paused, the pen hovering. His eyes traced the broken circle he had just drawn. Something about it throbbed in his vision, a pulse of meaning just out of reach.

"Daddy?"

The whisper came from behind him. Small, delicate. Lily's voice.

His heart lurched into his throat. He spun in his chair, papers scattering. The room was empty—only the door cracked slightly, hallway beyond swallowed in dark. His chest tightened as if he'd been caught mid-fall.

Slowly, Daniel turned back to the desk. The last circle on the page stared up at him, its fracture splitting wider than the others—as though the ink itself had torn open. He pressed his palm against it, trembling, half-expecting warmth.

Another rumble shook the window. Not thunder this time. Something deeper. Something waiting.

Daniel crumpled the page, clutched it in his fist, and let his forehead drop into his hand. "Lord," he whispered, voice shaking. "Answer me."

Outside, lightning split the sky, flooding the office with stark white light. For a breath, the broken circle burned across the wall as if carved into the plaster.

Then the light was gone.

And Daniel was alone again, with only the echo of his daughter's voice lingering in the silence.

The silence is not absence. It is waiting.

Chapter 1: The Celebration

A week after commencement, the banner still hung crooked over the back porch, sagging between two nails like it had exhaled: CONGRATULATIONS, DR. CROSS. The spring air held that damp Virginia softness that makes everything smell like cut grass and rain remembered. Paper plates clattered. Someone put a pitcher of sweet tea down hard enough to set the ice chiming. It wasn't a party so much as a lingering—family, two neighbors who'd helped Emily with extra chairs, a couple of Daniel's students who had ignored his protests and shown up anyway with store-bought brownies.

Emily moved through the small, bright house with a double portion of ease, barefoot, hair pulled back, one hand always finding Lily's shoulder or Daniel's elbow as if checking that they were real. Lily—seven, gap-toothed grin, Bun-Bun dangling from one arm by a threadbare ear—made a game of ferrying napkins to anyone who stood still long enough. Every so often she'd tug on Daniel's sleeve and whisper, "You're a doctor now," like it was a spell that might make him taller before her eyes.

He laughed, felt the laugh land inside his ribs and settle. A week ago he had walked across a stage under Liberty's bright lights, applauded into a degree that had felt both inevitable and unlikely. Today the degree lived as a frame on the bookshelf and as the way Emily kept looking at him when she thought he wasn't looking—pride under caution, love under fatigue, the old dance they'd learned after grief.

"Toast," someone said. It might have been one of the students; it might have been the neighbor with the sun hat and the firm opinions about azaleas. Heads turned. A plastic cup migrated toward his hand like an usher with a sense of ceremony.

Daniel stood. The porch boards had a give to them he liked, a barely-there swing underfoot that made even his body feel a little less like an argument with gravity. He cleared his throat. Words came easily to him when they wore footnotes. Here, under a sagging banner, with summer gnawing at the edges of spring and Emily resting her palm on Lily's crown as if blessing were a thing you could assign by touch, the words arrived and had opinions.

"Thank you," he began, and waited for the simple thing in him to be enough. "For being here, for making the ordinary feel like something we'll remember." He lifted the cup toward Emily. "For this woman who took on a man who thinks too much and never once asked for a refund."

Laughter, gentle and deserved.

"And to Lily," he said, and Lily stood on her toes, delighted by the way a name could change a room. "Who believes in magic more than I do and is usually right."

He should have stopped there. Instead the part of his mind that sharpened everything picked up the chalk. "You know the word doctor comes from docere—to teach," he heard himself say, and he felt the porch tilt from celebration to seminar. "And theology... well, telos is an end, a purpose, the why of things." He glanced at the banner, at the cup, at the faces he loved. "I suppose my trouble has always been that I don't know how to stop asking why. Even here. Especially here."

Emily's eyes found his and softened that half inch that meant come back. He smiled, corrected course. "But sometimes," he said, and let his voice drop from lecturing to living, "sometimes the why is just that God is good and we get to stand under a crooked banner and eat too much potato salad." He raised the cup. "To grace that doesn't ask us to deserve it."

They drank. The porch breathed. Someone told a story about Daniel mispronouncing a Greek middle voice in his first year at Regent and the chorus of groans that had followed. Lily tugged his sleeve again. "What does telos taste like?" she whispered, stage-serious.

"Lemon cake," he whispered back, and she beamed because lemon cake sat five feet away under a gauzy cover and some mysteries, it turned out, could be solved.

Inside the house the Blessings Jar lived on the kitchen counter, squat and blue and lidded, a Mason jar that had been promoted to a sacrament. They'd started it after the worst year had ended without ending them. Each Sunday night they wrote one good thing on a slip of paper and fed the jar— small mercies and stubborn ones, a kindness from a stranger, a bill that turned out to be less than feared, a laugh that ambushed grief and got away with it. Tonight Lily fished the jar's lid off with ceremony. "It's a special day," she announced to no one and everyone. "We can do one now."

"Paper's by the stove," Emily said, rinsing strawberries, her voice the quiet of a woman who had made a home by hand. Daniel reached for a pen without thinking. His hand drew a circle and broke it with a swift line before he realized what he was doing. He stared at the mark on the scrap—the fractured loop he'd sketched a thousand times on napkins and syllabi margins with nothing to show for it but ink stains and an odd sense of being watched for doing it.

"Daddy?" Lily had her eyes on his hand, on the shape that had arrived there like a trespasser. "Is that a donut with a bite?"

He blinked, laughed, tore the paper and tossed the accidental symbol into the recycling before it could argue theology. "No bites tonight. Write 'lemon cake.'"

She did, tongue between her teeth the way she always did when letters marched, then folded the slip and slid it into the jar with a thunk. Emily's slip followed, neat cursive. Daniel wrote This—us—here, folded the words until they were private, and fed the jar something that felt like a promise.

The students left. The neighbor carried her sun hat home like a prize. The porch banner sagged lower and became less a declaration than a fact. After the dishes were stacked and the last glass surrendered its ring of lemonade to the sink, the house contracted to the size of itself: three bedrooms; a hallway that believed in nightlights; a dining table that had weathered bills and birthdays without complaint. Lily brushed her teeth and argued half-heartedly with Bun-Bun about bedtime. "Bun-Bun says doctors don't have to sleep," she informed them.

"Bun-Bun is a known liar," Emily said, kissing her forehead. "Goodnight, moon-rocket."

"Goodnight, shortcake," Daniel added, and let himself be pulled into an embrace that smelled like strawberry toothpaste and girl.

He lingered in the doorway after the lamp clicked off, that old ache rising—not new and not gone, a tide that came twice a day no matter what weather he told himself he'd arranged. On the dresser, the small river stone they'd picked from the Shenandoah on last summer's Old Rag trip lay as it always did: smooth, the size of a bent thumb, an ordinary thing made necessary by the way Lily liked to carry it in her pocket like a talisman. He put his hand on it and felt, for a second, the implicit covenant of a father touching a world he can't fix and agreeing not to stop trying anyway.

"Hey," Emily said softly from the hallway. "Come back to the land of the living."

He did. In the kitchen they wiped counters and let the quiet grow in the corners like a friendly cat. The Blessings Jar glowed faintly under the cabinet light; blue gone to darker blue. "You know," Emily said, flicking a stray crumb into her palm and then into the sink, "for someone who says he doesn't know how to stop asking why, your toast wasn't half bad."

He grinned, leaned against the counter beside her. "It would have been better if I hadn't tried to teach Latin to a plastic cup."

"I like you better when you're teaching the difference between ordinary and sacred," she said, bumping his hip with hers. "Like lemon cake."

"Telos tastes like lemon cake," he agreed. "We should put that on a T-shirt."

Her smile thinned with tenderness. "You can… let yourself be happy, you know. A week. A night. This hour."

He nodded because he wanted to be the man who could. "I know." He watched a drop of water quiver at the lip of the faucet and fall. "I'm trying."

She reached, smoothed his collar with two fingers like she was ironing a crease out of something more important than fabric. "You don't have to solve us," she said. "You just have to sit in us."

After she slept, he stayed up because mind and habit had a pact. The house made its small nighttime sounds: a tick under the refrigerator, the HVAC's gentle exhale, the heater in the hallway clicking as it forgot and remembered. He sorted through cards with congratulations, through a note from his chair at Regent that managed to be both warm and a reminder of fall syllabi. A moth hurled itself at the porch light, a small insistence played out on the other side of the glass.

At 3:07 the microwave clock blinked on as if someone had just plugged it in, then steadied. The number found him with the accuracy of an old friend and an old wound. The air in the kitchen felt denser, the way air feels before you say something you'll have to live with. He flexed his hand and realized his palm held ink—half a circle traced there without his noticing, a moon bitten, a door ajar.

"Daddy?"

The word stood up from the dark behind him, small and unmarred.

He turned so fast his chair bit the floor. The doorway was empty. The hallway was nightlight and shadow. A few seconds passed. He knew this because the microwave said so.

"Lily?" he whispered, already sure. He went to her room anyway. She lay on her side, fists tucked under her chin in a barricade against dreams that thought they were bigger than they were. Bun-Bun stared at the ceiling with one eye more earnest than the other. The river stone gleamed faintly on the dresser as if it had been thinking.

He touched her hair. The small, constant miracle of a child not waking when a parent puts a hand between her and the world almost undid him. On the wall, the framed print of the verse Emily had picked years ago—He will cover you with His feathers, and under His wings you will find refuge—wore its letters like a promise that didn't need his permission to be true.

In the hallway he paused. The nightlight made the baseboards into white threads. Somewhere under the house or over it, thunder remembered how to be distant. He whispered a prayer that had not yet learned to be eloquent. Keep. Near. Please. He did not wait for an answer because he was a man who wanted answers too much already.

Back in the kitchen, he reached to turn off the over-sink light and the bulb popped with a crack that jerked his spine. Glass dusted the counter. The room went dark and then not—the nightlight's soft square and the microwave's green numerals remade the world small enough to hold. He stood very still and told his heart to come home.

The Blessings Jar held its blue quietly. He put the broom away without using it and decided that was what tomorrow was for. In the doorway to the hall he stopped again, listening to a silence that felt like a held breath, like someone about to speak.

Later, when he lay beside Emily and sleep came for him with slow hands, he saw the porch banner in his mind and the way doctor had been a brave word and a silly one at once. He promised God and himself and the room that he could learn to sit in joy without dissecting it. He would learn—he was sure of this—that some questions are doors that do not love you back.

Outside, the wind lifted once, laid itself down, and waited.

Chapter 2: The Questioning Heart

The house was quiet after dinner. Emily sorted laundry in the living room while Daniel sat at the kitchen table, his Bible and a half-read stack of theology books spread out before him. Lily colored at his feet, humming to herself as she sketched a picture of Bun-Bun surrounded by swirling, unfamiliar symbols.

Daniel glanced at the clock—10:27 p.m. He'd lost another hour to reading, chasing an answer he couldn't quite articulate. For days now, sleep felt distant. His mind, always restless, buzzed with questions about evil and suffering, the unseen battles he'd lectured about, and the shapes in Lily's art that unnerved him more than he cared to admit.

Emily returned, folding towels with sharp, precise movements. "You're a million miles away, Dan."

He managed a smile. "Just working on my next lecture."

She sat across from him, worry etched deep in her eyes. "I know you. You're not just working. What's really wrong?"

Daniel wanted to say it was nothing, just stress, just the ordinary pressures of family and faith. But the truth pressed in: the sleepless nights, the sense of being watched, the certainty that questions—real, heavy questions—were circling closer.

He hesitated, then reached for Lily's drawing. "Does this look... strange to you?"

Emily studied it—shapes like eyes, twisted loops, a faceless figure in the background. "She says she dreams them. Maybe she's just... imaginative."

But Daniel's heart pounded, remembering the crow, the chill, and the sense that something was moving in the corners of his life.

—

That night, Daniel lay awake beside Emily, haunted by memories he rarely let surface.

He was six years old again, standing on the back porch of a run-down house in rural Kentucky, suitcase in hand, his parents arguing inside. The fight ended in the crack of a screen door—his father stormed out, his mother silent and cold.

The next morning, Daniel was alone. No note, no goodbye. He waited, then wandered, hungry and frightened, until a neighbor called the authorities.

Years passed in foster homes—strangers' kindness and strangers' rage. Daniel grew wary, searching for belonging, always hoping his parents would come back. They never did.

But at thirteen, in a dusty church basement, a youth pastor named Joe handed Daniel a Bible. Joe spoke of a God who didn't abandon, a love that didn't quit.

Daniel had listened, arms folded, daring God to prove Himself. That night, on his borrowed cot, Daniel whispered a prayer—half plea, half accusation: "If you're real, I need to know why all this happened."

A strange peace came over him. Not answers, not yet—but the first flicker of hope, the sense that he was seen, known, even in his pain.

—

Daniel blinked, the memory burning bright. He looked at Emily sleeping, at Lily's form outlined in moonlight across the hall. Even now, all these years later, the questions hadn't left him. He was still that searching, abandoned boy—only now, he wore the mask of husband, father, professor.

A chill swept through him, making him pull the blanket tight.

Down the hall, Lily's soft voice drifted through the dark: "Good night, Willow."

Daniel sat up, heart pounding. There was no one named Willow in their home.

He crept to her door and peeked in. Lily was asleep, Bun-Bun clutched tight, a new drawing beside her on the pillow— circles, eyes, a figure with outstretched arms.

Daniel shivered, unable to shake the feeling that old wounds—and old questions—were closer than ever.

Chapter 3: Circles and Signs

July's heat arrived heavy, pressing down like a hand that wouldn't lift. For the Cross family, the middle of summer always meant one thing: the Old Rag hike. It wasn't just exercise. It was ritual. A pilgrimage, even, though Daniel never spoke of it that way. He liked to think of it as the one tradition untouched by his questions.

The morning of the trip, the house buzzed with nervous excitement. Daniel loaded the car with packs, bottled water, sunscreen, and Emily's trail mix, while Lily danced circles around him, Bun-Bun dangling by an ear from her small hand. Her "adventure stone," smooth and gray, rode safely in her pocket. Emily hummed as she double-checked lunches, her tension hidden behind efficiency. Before stepping out the door, she pressed her hand against the frame and whispered a prayer, the same blessing she always did before family trips. Lily copied her, palm against the wood, eyes shut tight.

Daniel lingered, feeling the prayer pull at him. He touched the frame too, but where Emily found reassurance, he found only silence.

The drive wound through Virginia farmland. Golden fields. Red barns with peeling paint. Fences sagging like tired bones. Lily pressed her forehead to the window, naming shapes in the clouds. "That one looks like Bun-Bun if he had wings. That one's a pancake. That one's... an angel."

Emily laughed, but the sound carried an edge. Daniel kept his hand on the wheel, the other in his pocket where the stone Emily had given him rested. He traced its edges, as if it could anchor him.

"Are angels always watching?" Lily asked suddenly.

Emily reached back, brushing her daughter's hair. "Yes, sweetheart. Always."

Daniel wanted to agree, but the words stuck in his throat. He had taught entire courses on angelology, lectured about messengers and guardians. And yet, he felt the question scrape raw against his heart.

The trail began gently, winding through shaded woods. Cicadas screamed their endless chorus, and damp earth gave off the tang of moss and decay. Lily darted ahead, stopping to collect rocks, each one deemed part of her "prayer collection." She asked question after question: Why do some trees fall while others stand? Do rocks remember the people who step on them? Do trees dream when no one looks?

Daniel tried to answer, but theology stumbled in the face of a seven-year-old's curiosity. Emily laughed softly. "You don't have to answer everything, Dan."

He smiled, though unease gnawed at him. She didn't understand—he did have to. Questions were the map of his life, and he feared the day he found one with no answer.

Halfway up, they rested on a boulder. Emily unpacked sandwiches, and Lily arranged her stones into a circle. Carefully, she placed a jagged one in the center.

"What's this one, honey?" Daniel asked, crouching beside her.

Lily's expression grew serious. "It's special. Willow says it keeps us safe."

Emily stiffened but said nothing. Daniel forced a chuckle. "Your friend Willow seems very wise."

"She is." Lily traced the circle with her finger. "She says angels glow different when they're sad. Like nightlights when they break."

Emily and Daniel exchanged a look. A silent conversation passed between them: Is this imagination? Or something else?

The climb grew harder, rock scrambling demanding hands and knees. Lily squealed with delight as she scrambled up, Daniel lifting her from behind, Emily guiding from above. Sweat stung his eyes, but joy mingled with exhaustion. At last, they neared the summit.

That's when Lily ran ahead and stopped cold in a small clearing. Daniel's chest tightened until he saw her—safe, unharmed—but then his gaze fell to what she was staring at.

Stones, arranged in a perfect circle around the base of an ancient oak. Carvings covered them: spirals, slashes, eyes. The air changed. Sound dimmed. Light bent strangely, as though filtered through water. Daniel's pulse quickened.

"Did you do this?" His voice sounded harsher than he intended.

Lily shook her head, eyes wide. "It was already here. Willow says it's old."

Emily caught up, pulling Lily close instinctively. "Dan... let's keep moving."

But Daniel crouched, hand hovering over a spiral. The stone was impossibly cold. When he touched it, his fingers recoiled as if from heat. For a moment, he swore the carving turned beneath his skin.

He snapped a photo with his phone, hands trembling.

At the summit, fog swirled around them, the valley below smudged in green and gray. Lily spread her arms wide, queen of the mountain. "We should do this forever," she declared. Then, softer, almost to herself: "What if this is our last trip?"

Emily hugged her fiercely. Daniel smiled, but it felt wrong on his face. He looked out at the valley and felt it again—that tilt, that presence just beyond sight. Watching. Waiting.

That night, the house was quiet again. Emily tucked Lily into bed, prayed over her, and left the nightlight glowing. Daniel sat with his phone, scrolling through photos. Trees, smiles, laughter. Then the clearing.

The screen flickered. For one second, the stone circle blurred into something else—a ring of eyes, wide and watching. He blinked, heart hammering. The image vanished, replaced by a blank gray square.

He refreshed. Nothing. The photo was gone.

From down the hall, Lily's laughter floated too loud, too sharp. She was supposed to be asleep. Daniel's hand trembled as he set the phone down.

The silence around him pressed close. Not empty. Waiting.

Chapter 4: Whispers in the Night

August arrived as if the world were exhaling. The lush green of summer dulled into softer shades, and mornings carried a whisper of coolness that hinted at the season's turn. Regent's brick walkways were scattered with the first dry leaves, a reminder that nothing stayed vibrant forever.

Daniel stood in front of his theology class, chalk dust staining his fingertips. He should have been steady here—in his element, guiding students through the mysteries of Scripture. But lately, his lectures slipped from his grasp. Words wandered. His once razor-sharp clarity blurred into speculation.

On the margins of his lecture notes, spirals bloomed unbidden. Circles with fractures. Eye-shapes staring back at him. He would catch himself tracing them mid-discussion, only to look up at rows of uneasy faces.

"Some knowledge," he said one morning, voice low and strange, "isn't meant to be chased. Some doors, once opened, cannot be shut."

A girl in the front row scribbled furiously, her brow creased. Others exchanged glances, uncertain if this was part of the syllabus or something else entirely. Daniel forced a smile, dismissed class early, and left to the rustle of whispers.

At home, shadows clung longer to the corners of rooms. Emily folded laundry with a precision that bordered on ritual, her movements tighter, more brittle. She lingered at Lily's doorway at night, hand on the frame, listening. Daniel would watch her from down the hall, the curve of her shoulders outlined in lamplight, and know she was searching for sounds she didn't want to find.

Lily's dreams had grown stranger. One evening, Emily confided as she stacked dishes into the dishwasher. "She said she saw Willow again," she whispered, her voice thin with strain. "Willow taught her a song, Dan. When I asked what it sounded like…" Emily's hands stopped midair, plate dripping suds. "…she just said, 'It's for the night, not the day.'"

Daniel said nothing, but unease dug deeper into him.

That night, the music came.

It began faint, like a string plucked in another room. A melody without rhythm, sorrowful and hypnotic, weaving through the house. Daniel woke with his heart racing, the clock on the nightstand glaring 3:07 a.m.. He slipped from bed, padding silently down the hall.

Lily's door was ajar, light spilling from her nightlight in a golden wedge across the floorboards. Inside, she slept peacefully, Bun-Bun under her chin, lips moving faintly as if whispering prayers in a tongue Daniel couldn't decipher.

The music lingered, but now he couldn't tell if it came from her or the walls themselves.

When he reached his office, the notepad on his desk was already filled—page after page of the Old Rag symbol. He didn't remember drawing them. His hand ached as though he'd been writing for hours. He sat, breath shallow, and began searching online archives.

Celtic knots. Norse runes. Angelic sigils. Revelation's apocalyptic seals. Nothing matched. Every trail ended in dead links and scholars muttering about "lost languages" and "forgotten mysteries." His chest tightened.

Desperate, he emailed his old professor, Dr. Everett, attaching a photo of the drawing. The reply came the next day: Never seen anything quite like it. Why do you ask?

Daniel typed, erased, typed again. He never hit send.

That afternoon, the mail brought a letter. No return address. Plain white envelope. He nearly tossed it aside with the bills, but something in its weight stopped him.

Inside: a single blank sheet of paper.

He turned it over, squinted, ran his fingers across it. Nothing. Then, heart thudding, he rummaged through the junk drawer until he found the UV flashlight.

The page erupted in violet light—the symbol. The same circle, the same fracture, glowing as though alive.

Daniel dropped the paper. His eyes darted to the kitchen clock. 3:07 p.m.

That night, the dream came.

He was back at Old Rag. The air was thick, still, as though sound itself were forbidden. He stood within the stone circle, unable to move, his chest compressed by unseen weight. Shadows pressed closer, watching.

A voice rose—soft, infinite, threaded with sorrow.

"Some doors, once opened, cannot be closed."

The words vibrated through his bones. He tried to pray, but his lips wouldn't move.

He woke to Emily shaking him, her face pale, her hands trembling.

"Dan... she was talking in her sleep again." Her voice broke. "She said Willow was outside. And she said... she said the song is almost finished."

Daniel pulled her close, feeling the shiver in her frame. Together, they listened. The house around them seemed to breathe, walls holding their own quiet rhythm.

Neither of them slept again that night.

Chapter 5: The Fraying Edge

September crept in with a cool bite to the morning air, the kind that hinted at sweaters and woodsmoke even while summer leaves clung stubbornly to the branches. At Regent University, Daniel gripped the podium with white-knuckled hands, his notes a blur of ink and indecipherable scratches.

He should have been steady here. This was his domain. Yet the lecture unraveled the moment he opened his mouth.

"…spiritual warfare," he began, voice hollow, "is not… not metaphor." His throat caught. "It's closer than we think. Closer than…"

Students exchanged uneasy looks. A boy in the back shifted, folding his arms. A girl in the second row scribbled frantically, as if his fragmented sentences held secrets. Another stifled a laugh, then covered it with a cough.

Daniel's eyes drifted to the margins of his notes. Spirals. Eyes. Circles fractured by invisible hands. He didn't remember drawing them. He rubbed at the paper as though friction alone could erase their presence.

"We'll... pick this up next week," he muttered. He shut the Bible with a snap, the sound echoing too loud in the stunned room. Students filed out, whispering. None looked him in the eye.

At home, Emily was pulling chicken from the freezer when something dark on the carpet caught her eye.

A small bird lay perfectly still beneath the spill of late sunlight, wings folded neatly, eyes glassy and black.

Her stomach dropped. The doors were locked. The windows latched. No way in. Yet here it was.

"Daniel!" Her voice cracked.

He appeared in the doorway, tie crooked, eyes shadowed. "What is it?"

She pointed wordlessly.

His jaw tightened as he crouched. "It's just... it's just a bird." He said it too quickly.

Emily's hands shook. "How did it get inside?"

No answer. He wrapped the bird in a dish towel, carried it to the oak tree, and buried it in silence.

That night, when he dreamed, the bird's eyes gleamed in the dark, watching him from the soil.

Two days later, Emily woke to the creak of the back door. Panic shot through her. She bolted from bed, bare feet on cold floor, rushing down the hallway.

Outside, in the silver predawn, Lily stood barefoot in the grass, dew soaking her nightgown. She looked up at the stars as though waiting for them to speak.

"Lily!" Emily's voice broke as she scooped her daughter into a blanket. "What are you doing?"

"Willow wanted me to see the stars," Lily whispered sleepily. She opened her small fist, revealing a pale, smooth stone etched with looping marks—the same marks Daniel had been obsessing over for weeks.

Emily's breath caught. She crushed her daughter against her chest, whispering fiercely, "No more night walks. Not ever."

Sunday evening, the Blessings Jar sat in its place of honor at the dinner table. The ritual had always been joy—paper slips folded with thanks, laughter spilling between the cracks.

Not this time.

Lily fiddled with Bun-Bun's ears. Emily stared at her empty slip of paper. Daniel scrawled something quickly, unwilling to share.

Emily reached for the jar.

The glass split with a violent crack, shattering down the middle. The sound ripped through the room like a gunshot. Slips of paper spilled across the table, gratitude scattered like autumn leaves.

Lily screamed.

Emily dropped the jar, shards glittering against the wood. "I—I didn't—"

Daniel stared; throat dry, unable to move.

Through sobs, Lily whispered: "Willow says the jar broke because Daddy's not listening."

That night, Daniel couldn't stay away from his office. The desk was strewn with Lily's drawings—rings within rings, faceless figures, eyes peering from the margins. His own notebook was filled with frantic sketches, layered symbols that blurred into one another.

"You're close," a voice whispered.

He froze.

The desk lamp flickered, sputtering into shadows. The whisper brushed his ear like a cold wind: "Keep searching."

His chest seized. He turned sharply, but the room was empty, corners deeper than they should have been.

The lamp hummed once, then died.

Heart pounding, Daniel grabbed his bag and fled down the hall. Lights above him flickered, chasing him like dying stars.

In the car, he jammed the key into the ignition. The engine coughed, headlights slicing the night. The dashboard clock glowed steady: 3:07.

The radio hissed alive without his touch. Static swelled into a voice—low, distorted, unmistakable.

It whispered his name.

Chapter 6: The Erosion

October arrived on a breath you could see. The mornings were crisp and white-edged, each exhale a ghost. Maple leaves burned out along the neighborhood, and the wind carried that sweet rot of endings. In the Cross house, the air felt thinner, as if the walls had learned to listen.

Daniel told himself the semester's rhythm would steady him. He stacked notes, smoothed syllabi, pulled on the professor's voice he'd worn for years. The drive to Regent—forty-five minutes if the lights favored him—should have been soul-clearing country and radio hymns. Instead, he watched the road with a hunter's focus, catching flashes in the treeline: a tall shadow slipping between trunks, a pale oval where no face should be. Each time he turned, there was nothing but trees and his own reflection in the glass.

Campus didn't fix it. In the lecture hall, chalk dust rose in thin halos beneath the fluorescents, and his mouth kept forming words that felt like someone else's. He taught Ephesians and the armor of God, and the sentence snagged on his tongue—we wrestle not against flesh and blood—because lately, he wasn't sure what any of this was against. A girl in the second row asked about principalities; Daniel's answer unraveled into a story about doors you shouldn't open. Half the class leaned forward. The rest shifted in their seats and looked at the clock.

He lost an hour between the classroom and his office and found mud drying on his shoes. No memory of leaving the building. Faint ink crawled along the inside of his forearm; the ghost of a spiral he didn't remember drawing. He scrubbed at it until the skin went raw.

Back home, Emily folded the day into neat, square routines—the way she did when storms gathered—laundry sorted, lesson plans checked, pantry organized so tightly Daniel couldn't find the sugar. She was gentle with Lily and careful with him, the space between careful and fearful narrowing by the day.

Lily grew quiet. The humming he'd teased her for became a thread of sound too small for daylight. She didn't draw in front of him anymore; he'd find the pages later, tucked under her mattress or between the couch cushions—rings within rings, eyes like seeds.

One night he caught her speaking softly in the hallway, facing the dark.

"Who are you talking to, baby?" he asked.

She blinked as if waking. "No one," she said, then whispered, "It's crowded at night."

That same week, Father Grayson left a message: If you want me to stop by—pray with you, just talk—I'm here. You don't need to carry everything yourself. Daniel stared at his reflection in the mirror and hit delete with his elbow.

He stayed late on campus after that, burying himself in the stacks where the old books lived—apocrypha, angelology, medieval demonologies that felt silly by day and like field guides after dusk. He copied symbols until they knotted together like vines. The circle from Old Rag hovered in his mind and refused to land on paper. When he finally stumbled to his car, the dashboard clock seemed to wait for him—3:07. The radio hissed to life without his touch. Static shaped a voice that could have been his own, speaking his name.

The house learned to speak in October.

Footsteps padded down the hall when everyone should have been asleep. The bathroom faucet turned itself on to a thin thread that stopped the moment a hand reached for it. Lily's room smelled of damp earth each morning, as if the garden had crept inside and stretched out on her rug.

"I'm taking her to sleep in our bed tonight," Emily said, jaw set.

Daniel nodded and didn't say what he was thinking: the smell was in their room too, faint under the cotton and coffee and cinnamon.

They tried to braid faith through the fear. Emily's Bible lived on the kitchen counter now, open to Psalms. When the wind cuffed the house and the windows rattled, she'd lay her palm flat on the page like a seal. She prayed aloud when she thought she was alone. Daniel heard her sometimes, steady low murmurs over the sink—In peace I will both lie down and sleep—and felt both grateful and ashamed.

The clocks joined in. Not just digital, but the kitchen wall clock, the oven, the bedside alarm. Each night they paused at 3:07. Not a flicker—paused. Hands and red segments held in a minute so taut Daniel felt it in his teeth. When the house resumed, he and Emily looked up at the same time and pretended they hadn't noticed.

"Take a weekend," she said bravely. "No books. No notes. Let's drive somewhere quiet. We could go back to the mountains. Just us. Break whatever this is."

He kissed her temple and said, "Let me get through midterms." Her mouth made a little line he recognized from the mirror.

That night, Lily dreamed. A meadow sharper than reality, a willow shimmering with moonlight, and a figure light as breath on a winter morning.

"Little one," the figure said, "are you ready to leave earth?"

Lily clutched Bun-Bun. "Do I have to?"

"Not yet. But the song is almost finished."

She whispered, "I don't want to leave Mommy. Or Daddy."

"Then stay close to the light. The darkness is growing bold."

When she woke, she climbed into bed with them trembling. In the morning she said, "The angel told me the light is already in the house." Daniel set his coffee down very carefully.

He and Emily argued in whispers.

"She's seven," Emily said. "She shouldn't be talking about leaving. She shouldn't smell dirt in her bedroom. She shouldn't be afraid to sleep where she feels… crowded."

"I'm not dismissing it," Daniel said, hating the defensiveness. "I'm trying to understand it."

"She doesn't need you to understand it," Emily said softly. "She needs you to be her dad."

That night the footsteps paused outside their door, the way Lily did when deciding whether to climb in. When Daniel opened it, the hallway was only carpet and photos. But Lily's drawing tacked to the wall had changed: the ring of eyes that had been closed were now open.

In the morning, the smell of damp leaves followed them into the kitchen. Daniel wrote a message to Father Grayson and erased it. He stared at a search bar until his eyes watered, then filled it with words for seal.

The clocks stopped again at 3:07. Emily reached for his hand in the dark and found it. He held on.

When he tucked Lily in, she whispered, "Willow says the song is almost finished. The night song. The one that tells the house who to let in."

Down the hall, the Bible lay open on the counter. A wind hummed in the eaves, a note that wasn't a note, the sound of a house practicing a new language. Daniel stood in the doorway after the light was off, listening. Somewhere in the dark, someone was humming. It wasn't Emily. It wasn't Lily. For one blasphemous moment, he thought it might be the house itself.

The minute slipped toward the one that never wanted to end.

Chapter 7: Shattered Routine

November bled in with frost at the edges of the mornings, a quiet chill that found its way through the house no matter how high Emily turned the thermostat. The trees outside stood bare, black fingers scratching at a slate-gray sky. Inside, the air thickened with the silence of a house that had learned to hold its breath.

Daniel told himself routine could be armor. He rose early, pressed ties flat against his chest, packed his bag with syllabi and half-finished notes, then drove the winding hour to Regent University. The road, lined with skeletal trees and shadow-patched fields, felt less like a commute and more like a narrowing corridor. The radio whispered static more often than hymns now, and sometimes he swore it shaped syllables that could almost be his name.

In the lecture hall, the mask slipped. He began with scripture, with Paul's words about powers and principalities, but his hand betrayed him. Where an outline should have been, spirals bloomed across the whiteboard—loops, ribs, broken circles. His chalk screeched faster, urgent, until the board was a fever of black shapes that connected only in desperation. His voice cracked, carrying words too sharp to pass for passion.

"Evil doesn't wait for permission," he told the silent room. "It finds the cracks."

A hand rose timidly near the back. "Professor Cross," a student asked, "are you... okay?"

The words didn't reach him. The whispers were louder— voices rustling like dry leaves, syllables layered in tones he half-recognized: his own voice, Emily's, Lily's. His marker clattered to the floor. He turned, hollow-eyed, and whispered a name—maybe Lily's, maybe not—before his legs gave way.

He woke later in the faculty office, throat raw, head pounding. The dean sat opposite; her hands folded too tightly in her lap. "We're... putting you on leave, Daniel. You need rest."

He nodded as if it made sense. Nothing did anymore.

By midweek, lectures were abandoned. His office became his burrow: blinds drawn; desk buried beneath Lily's drawings. Page after page of eyes and rings, repeating until they seemed to pulse if he stared long enough. The whispers found him there, too, slipping between the hum of the vents and the tick of the clock.

Emily called one evening, her voice as thin as the static on the radio. "You missed dinner again. Lily asked if you were mad at her."

His throat tightened. "Tell her I'll be home soon."

"Daniel…" Her whisper broke. "You're scaring her."

He didn't know how to answer. Because she was right.

The house had changed by the time he dragged himself back. At night, Lily sang in her sleep. Her lips didn't move, but the song threaded through the walls, a lullaby meant for someone else. Symbols faintly glowed on the kitchen tiles, etched themselves into the drywall of his office. He tried scrubbing once; the shapes bled back through, stubborn as scars.

Emily still tried. She lit candles at dinner, whispered blessings onto scraps of paper and tucked them into the cracked jar. Her hands trembled, but her voice stayed steady. Lily sat silent through these rituals; her wide eyes fixed on something that no one else could see.

It was past midnight when Daniel woke to the sound of footsteps in the hall. Slow, deliberate. He rose, his feet cold against the hardwood, and found Lily standing at the far end, Bun-Bun dangling from one hand, hair tangled with sleep.

"Lily?" His whisper cracked. "What are you doing up?"

She didn't answer at first. Then, in a calm voice that did not belong to her, she said, "Daddy, Willow says it's almost time."

She turned and padded back to her room, humming the endless song. Daniel didn't follow. He couldn't.

Later, in the kitchen, he sat alone under the weak light, surrounded by her drawings. Page after page of their family—smiling, together—but always with black shapes behind them, pressing closer with each stroke of crayon.

The clock ticked softly.

3:07.

And then silence.

The whole house held its breath.

Chapter 8: The Fractured Night

By late November, the cold had settled into the bones of the house. It wasn't just the draft seeping through the windows or the bite of morning frost. It was in the air itself—still, heavy, the kind of quiet that felt aware. Even the radiators groaned less, as if they, too, were afraid to speak.

Daniel rarely left anymore. His office had become both refuge and cage, walls papered with Lily's drawings and his own frantic scrawl. Notebook pages sprawled across the desk, coffee cups stacked like sentries, ink staining his fingers. He traced symbols until his knuckles cramped, each spiral more tangled than the last, convinced that if he just pressed harder, stared longer, some key would unlock. The truth never did.

Emily's footsteps became prayers. She moved from room to room, murmuring scripture under her breath, the old leather Bible clutched like a shield. She prayed over Lily at night, her voice unsteady, weaving verses as though stitching patches of light into the dark corners. Sometimes Daniel stood in the doorway, watching her lips move. Sometimes he hated her for her steadiness. Sometimes he loved her for not breaking. Always, he felt the gulf widening between them.

And Lily… Lily had grown solemn. The chatter and constant humming were gone. When she did hum, the sound froze

Daniel mid-scribble, his pen hovering above paper. The tune was never quite recognizable, always caught between lullaby and dirge, carrying weight too old for a child.

Daniel's nights were worse. When sleep came, it came like a fall, dragging him into visions too solid to be dreams.

He walked the forest near Old Rag, the earth cold beneath his bare feet, trees whispering words just out of reach. The mountain rose before him, crowned with light and shadow that spiraled endlessly upward. Emily and Lily stood in the clearing ahead, their eyes empty, their mouths moving in prayer he couldn't hear. Behind them the stone circle pulsed with dim light.

At its center stood a figure—tall, faceless, unmoving. The silence around it screamed.

Daniel always woke at 3:07, drenched in sweat, mouth metallic with copper. Back in the dim of his office, faint marks streaked his arms and wrists—symbols written in trembling lines he never remembered making. Some nights he scrubbed until his skin turned raw. The ink always returned.

Emily fought to hold them together with rituals—Saturday pancakes, the Blessings Jar, bedtime prayers whispered into

Lily's hair. But rituals frayed. Their meaning slid through her fingers like water.

One night, standing in the kitchen with her hands flat on the counter, she broke. "You have to stop," she whispered, trembling. "Stop with the books, the drawings. Stop pretending you can fix this."

Daniel looked up; eyes hollow.

"Look at me, Dan." Her voice cracked. "You're losing yourself. And you're losing us with you."

"I'm trying," he rasped. "I'm trying to protect you. To protect her. There's something here, Emily. Answers. If I can just—"

"Answers won't stop this!" she snapped, then clamped her hand over her mouth, horrified at her own volume.

From the doorway, a smaller voice cut the room in half: "It won't stop until the song is done."

Lily stood there, Bun-Bun dangling from her hand, her gaze far beyond both of them. Neither parent spoke.

In the days that followed, Lily grew stranger. She sat barefoot in the backyard despite the cold, her breath small puffs of frost. She arranged prayer stones in perfect circles, each one aligned with uncanny precision. When Emily asked what she was doing, Lily tilted her head.

"Willow says the house will be quiet soon."

She turned back to her stones, humming softly, as if her answer was already complete.

The night it all fractured began like any other. Dinner in silence. Emily clearing plates with brittle care. Lily's humming threading faintly through the walls. The wind clawed against the windows, but the rooms themselves were still, listening.

At 3:07, the lights flickered once and died. Darkness swallowed the house, thick and total.

The hum grew louder. Not a single note but a braid of voices, whispers layered into melody. It crawled along Daniel's skin, vibrated in his teeth. He moved through the house slowly, each step cautious against the hardwood that felt colder than stone. The air pressed heavy, charged, as faint symbols pulsed on the walls, glowing like veins under skin.

Emily woke to find him standing in the living room, rigid, eyes fixed on the glowing patterns. His hands trembled at his sides, as if pulled between reaching and recoiling.

"Dan?" Her whisper broke.

He didn't answer.

From the hallway came the soft pad of bare feet. Lily appeared, hair hanging in her face, Bun-Bun limp in her grip. She looked so small, and yet her voice filled the room with calm certainty:

"Willow says the song is over."

Silence pressed in, thick as earth.

When dawn crept through the blinds, the power returned, lights humming back to life as if nothing had happened. But the house was not the same. Hollow. Waiting.

Daniel sat at the kitchen table, Lily's drawings fanned before him—family portraits smiling under a sky gone black, shadow-shapes crowding closer with each page. His pen hovered above one, as if he could change the outcome by adding another line. He didn't.

Emily stood at the counter, Bible clutched tight, her whispered prayer breaking against the silence.

"Lord," she breathed, voice a thread fraying under strain, "keep us. Please... keep us."

And the silence listened.

Chapter 9: Admission

The week after Lily said the song was over, the house stopped pretending to be a house.

Daniel barely slept. He moved from room to room as if patrolling a perimeter only he could see, whispering fragments of prayers that collapsed into broken words. His office turned into a nest of paper—every surface buried under circles, spirals, and eyes that refused to meet in sense. He pressed pens until they bled dry, then scored the paper with the empty nib, as if carving meaning could force it to exist.

Emily found him on the kitchen floor before dawn, knees pulled tight, surrounded by drawings like fallen leaves. He whispered in the rhythm of bedtime prayers, but the words had splintered—the Lord's Prayer dissolving into pleas about seals, doors, and a darkness that had learned their names.

"Dan." She knelt, cupping his cheeks. "Look at me."

He blinked, surfacing wrong, like a diver breaking too fast. For a heartbeat his eyes skated past her—as though something stood behind her. Then his gaze clutched hers and wouldn't let go.

"Help me," he rasped. The sound scraped her chest. "Please."

Emily's hands trembled as she reached for the phone.

The Intervention

Father Grayson arrived with two quiet men from church, both carrying the weary strength of people who had stood too often at midnight hospital doors. The house seemed to resist their entry; the air pressed back. Emily's Bible pages fluttered open on the side table though no window stirred.

They gathered in the living room. Candlelight drew fragile islands of warmth. Grayson placed a steadying hand on Daniel's shoulder.

"Lord, we ask Your covering. We ask Your peace. We ask Your light to drive out every shadow."

Daniel tried to follow, but the house had learned another liturgy. A low hum underpinned the priest's words—the same melody that had threaded through Lily's chest. It curled through the glassware, turning cups into tuning forks.

"Stop," Daniel choked, shaking his head. "Stop—do you hear it?" His eyes flicked to the churchmen. For one raw instant, their faces warped in the candlelight, eyes black as burned photographs.

He staggered up, knocking into the coffee table. Wax spilled; flame died. Smoke smudged the air.

Grayson didn't flinch. He pressed closer, forehead nearly to Daniel's. "Stay with me."

The hum rose like bees inside the walls.

Something inside Daniel gave way. He collapsed—not fainting, not sleeping, but folding as if the center pole had been pulled from a tent. Sobs ripped out of him, words of apology he couldn't name, a litany that might have been repentance or surrender.

Emily's hand shook as she made the call.

The Departure

The paramedics came soft-voiced, moving with the practiced reverence of people trained not to deepen humiliation. They asked Daniel his name, the date, the place. He got two right. He kept glancing at the ceiling where faint symbols pulsed like veins beneath plaster.

They fastened the restraints as if tucking in a child. Emily pressed her lips to his forehead, whispering she would follow. Grayson bent low, hand on Daniel's chest: "He won't leave you."

From the shadowed stairwell, Lily watched. Bun-Bun dangled loose in her hand. She didn't cry, didn't call. Her small voice drifted down like a lullaby.

"It's too late, Daddy. They're already here."

The words followed him into the night like a curse disguised as a blessing.

The ambulance was a box of light rolling through sleeping streets. Daniel stared at the straps across his chest, whispering Even though I walk... Even though I walk...

The paramedic beside him—tired eyes, soft mouth— hummed faintly.

"You hear it too?" Daniel asked, fear and hope tangled.

She blinked, startled. "Just a tune stuck in my head."

"What tune?"

Her brow furrowed. "Don't know. I can never remember it when I try."

The siren stayed silent. The tires whispered on blacktop. Daniel refused to look at the window—sometimes reflections there weren't his.

The Hospital

The sign outside softened the truth with a harmless name. Inside, it was fluorescent honesty: white walls, clipped voices, the hush of heavy doors.

They unbuckled him with the same competence they had fastened him. For a moment, he was a man again, not a package.

Paperwork multiplied. A nurse with gentle detachment checked vitals. "Do you feel like harming yourself or others?"

Daniel laughed, hollow. "I don't trust those definitions anymore."

"Dr. Harker will be your attending," the nurse said. "She's good."

The woman who entered carried calm like a shield. Dark hair pulled back, eyes the color of wet stone, posture so straight it made him notice his own slouch. She offered her hand.

"Daniel. I'm Dr. Elizabeth Harker."

Her palm was warm. The warmth stung his eyes.

"You've been carrying a great deal," she said. No pity, no smile. "We'll carry it together awhile."

They inventoried his pockets. ChapStick. A folded drawing of Lily's he didn't remember taking. His smooth prayer stone. They confiscated the first two. Let him keep the stone. He held it like an anchor.

The Unit

His room was a narrow rectangle: bed bolted down,
nightstand bolted down, a window too slim for view or
escape. Antiseptic stung his nose. The air tasted recycled.

From the doorway, he saw the unit breathe. A man shuffled
with folded hands. A woman sketched endlessly on the
linoleum. A tattooed giant rocked in a chair, muttering
scrambled Scripture. A pale girl in her twenties sat by the
wall, humming soundlessly, head tilted like she was listening
inside the plaster.

"Ava White," the nurse murmured, following his gaze. "She
keeps to herself."

Daniel couldn't stop staring. Something in the tilt of her head
echoed Lily at the window.

Dr. Harker returned, carrying a chair—unbolted—and set it
down facing him. She sat.

"No surprises here if we can help it," she said. "Tell the truth.
Eat what you can. Sleep when you can. And if you can't, tell
us that too."

He nodded, hollow.

"What do you hear right now?"

He listened: vents, footsteps, a hum stitched behind the paint.

"Music," he said. "Always music."

"Does it frighten you?"

"No." His throat tightened. "It feels... familiar."

She didn't write it down. "We'll talk more tomorrow."

The Dream

Night dropped. The unit dimmed to its steady thrum—the sound of a ship already committed to course. Daniel lay counting breaths until numbers lost meaning.

He dreamed of trees again. The Old Rag trail underfoot. The hospital stitched into the woods, beds under oaks, doors without walls. The stone circle glowed around him, humming with power.

Emily and Lily stood hand in hand, not looking at him. Their mouths shaped a name that wasn't his.

At the circle's edge stood the faceless figure, tall and patient.

And beyond it, Ava White watched him, head tilted in the same listening angle as Lily.

"Do you hear it?" Daniel asked.

Ava's lips parted. For a heartbeat the hum spiked, splitting the dream like glass under pressure.

She whispered, almost kindly: "I always have."

Daniel woke with the sound still ringing in his bones.

Chapter 10: The Quiet Between Walls

The mornings at the hospital were the same, every single one, like the world had been reset overnight. Lights snapped on at six, flooding the room with sterile brightness. Footsteps whispered along the corridor—soft soles on waxed linoleum, keys clinking faintly on belts. Breakfast trays rattled down the hall, their muted clatter swallowed by the hum of the intercom as it buzzed to life with the same scripted greeting.

Daniel hated how quickly the rhythm settled into his bones. Wake up. Line up for vitals. Pills at the nurse's station. Breakfast in the common room, all plastic utensils and lukewarm oatmeal. The same pattern, over and over, as though the routine was designed to make him forget the world outside—the one where Emily still left his coffee on the counter for a week before she stopped, where Lily's laughter used to fill the rooms.

He traced the edge of his prayer stone with his thumb, the worn grooves grounding him in a way nothing else did. Around him, the ward moved in quiet currents—some patients pacing, others staring at nothing. He memorized their faces, their patterns, the little ticks of their broken days.

Dr. Harker met with him every afternoon in her office, the room stripped down to its bones: one desk, two chairs, a muted clock ticking somewhere behind him. She didn't rush him, didn't push.

"Tell me what you see," she said one session, her hands folded loosely on her lap.

Daniel stared at the white wall for a long moment, the hum vibrating in the silence. "It's not just here," he whispered. "It's everywhere. The song... it doesn't stop."

"What song?" she asked softly.

"The one they hear," he said, almost to himself. "The one Lily knew before she could speak."

Dr. Harker didn't write anything down. She just watched him, eyes steady but unreadable. "And what do you think the song means, Daniel?"

He blinked; his mouth dry. "I think... I think it's calling something closer."

The patients fascinated him, and terrified him.

Ava sat in the corner of the common room most days, cross-legged with her back against the wall, humming. Always the same melody—low, quiet, and sharp enough to raise the hairs along Daniel's arms. The first time he stopped near her, she looked up with pale, unblinking eyes.

"They're here too," she said softly.

Daniel's throat tightened. "Who's here?"

She tilted her head, listening to something only she could hear. "The ones between the walls. They follow the sound."

Mick, the broad man with scripture inked across his arms, never stopped moving his lips. Psalm after Psalm, sometimes Revelation, muttered fast as if the words themselves were armor. When their eyes met across the common room one evening, Mick stopped mid-verse and said, almost conversationally, "The seals don't break on their own, you know. Someone has to open them."

Then he smiled. Too wide. Too knowing.

Sarah rarely spoke at all. She sat by the window in the group room, a dull pencil gripped in white-knuckled hands, sketching circles and lines on cheap paper. Daniel froze the

66

first time he saw them—identical to his own drawings. When he asked her where she'd seen them, she didn't look up.

"They find you," she said simply. "Always."

The nights were the worst.

At 3:07, the lights flickered. Not the casual hum-and-flicker of old wiring, but sharp, deliberate, as though something wanted to be sure he noticed. The humming started soft— like the vibration of a phone against wood—then grew louder, threading through the vents, the mattress, his bones.

Daniel pressed the pillow over his ears, but the sound wasn't in the room. It was inside him.

The staff acted like nothing happened. Security footage from the ward showed blank, unbroken minutes. The nurses smiled when he asked, patient but detached, like they'd been trained to be kind without getting too close.

During one session, he drifted.

One moment, Dr. Harker was speaking softly across the desk. The next, the world had slipped sideways. Her office melted away, walls dissolving into the dark sprawl of the forest near Old Rag. The hospital was there too, impossible and seamless, its white hallways stitched into the treeline, glowing faintly like veins.

Somewhere beyond the trees, Lily's voice called his name.

"Daniel," Dr. Harker said sharply, snapping him back, her hand gripping the arm of his chair. Her usually steady face was pale. "Breathe. With me. In… and out."

The room steadied, but the hum lingered in his chest long after the session ended.

Ava spoke to him more after that.

"You know it won't stop," she said one evening, sitting beside him in the common area. Her voice was soft, almost kind. "Walls don't keep them out. They never did."

Daniel turned to her slowly. "You hear it too."

She smiled faintly. "Everyone here does. Some just pretend they don't, so they can sleep at night."

Mick, pacing along the edge of the room, caught his eye again. His voice rose above the steady murmur of the ward: "When the song ends, so does the waiting. You know that, don't you?"

Daniel looked away.

That night, he couldn't sleep. The humming started early, quiet at first, almost soothing. But by 3:07, it had grown louder, vibrating the metal frame of his bed, pressing against his ribs.

He clutched the prayer stone in his fist until the edges dug into his skin, whispering a fractured prayer against the noise.

And just as the lights blinked out, plunging the room into darkness, the hum stopped.

In the silence that followed, a voice he knew too well—faint, almost tender—threaded through the black.

"They know you, Daniel. They've always known you."

Chapter 11: The Thin Veil

The ward learned his name without anyone saying it. Not the staff—they had known it from the file—but the ward itself, in the way the doors sighed when he passed and the vents breathed his temperature back to him. A few days in, the rhythm almost felt like mercy. Wake to fluorescents, vitals, paper cups with chalky moons inside, oatmeal that steamed without smelling like anything. Sit in the common room. Pretend the sameness could hold.

For a while, it did. The humming in his bones fell to a thread he could step over. He started showing up for groups, for meals, for the small polite rituals of a place built to keep time from turning into weather. He learned the staff by their footsteps, the patients by their silences. He nodded when people nodded. He slept—badly, briefly—but sleep came.

Dr. Harker's office carried its own weather: a square of pale light, a clock with a second hand that did not tick so much as lay the same line down again and again. She let quiet be quiet. When she asked him to talk, her voice didn't lead; it made room.

"Tell me about the symbols," she said one afternoon. "How you first saw them."

"In Lily's drawings," he said. "In my head before that, probably. In the woods. On the house. Now—" He lifted his hands. "If I look too long at anything white, I can talk myself into seeing the edges of them."

"And the song?"

He looked past her shoulder at the blank wall. "Sometimes it's there and sometimes it's pretending to be a vent."

"Do you believe it is external?" she asked gently. "Not produced by your mind?"

"I believe it's old," he said. "I believe it doesn't stop when I close my eyes."

She watched him a beat longer than comfort allowed. "Faith can be a map," she said. "It can also be a magnifying glass."

"Or armor," he said, before he could help it.

"Or armor," she allowed. "If fear is the weapon pointed at you, armor matters."

71

He left her office steadier than he'd entered, which wasn't the same as steady.

In the common room, the lives around him clinked and drifted. Ava sat in her corner with her knees up, palms flat on the tile, humming under her breath. It was Lily's melody slowed down until the notes could hide in the spaces between floors. When he paused beside her, she looked up the way a cat looks at a window it already knows.

"The quiet won't hold," she said.

"How long do we have?"

She tilted her head, listening to a distance he couldn't measure. "Until it doesn't."

Mick made circuits around the room, lips moving, scripture in a low spill that sounded like a man patching a boat as fast as he can. "Seal... trumpet... bowl..." The words wove in and out of sense. When he reached Daniel, he stopped and, without warning, grinned. "You draw like a priest at the wrong mass."

Daniel didn't know what to do with that, so he nodded as if he did.

Sarah held court with her paper and dull pencil near the window. Always circles. Always the same curved ribs of meaning. He forced himself to approach anyway. "Where did you see these first?"

She didn't look up. "I didn't," she said. "They saw me."

That evening the smell changed. It came in low and slow, so the mind could pretend it was memory: first rain and soil, then leaves, then the faint nick of iron at the back of the tongue. Earth, wet and metallic. A nurse propped a door, muttered about the HVAC. Security checked cameras for the flickers that kept turning up around dawn and found, once again, an immaculate stream of nothing.

He slept and fell. The forest met him like it had been waiting. Old Rag rose in a way that defied distance, and the hospital stitched along its flank like an addition no one had permitted. The stone circle glowed with its own cold, and inside it stood Lily with Bun-Bun crooked under her arm. Her mouth moved—Daddy—but the sound came through like speech underwater. When he reached for her, her eyes darkened, not evil, not empty—covered, like a mirror pressed with a hand. "It's almost over, Daddy," she mouthed, and then the hand lifted and she was gone.

He woke with the sheet twisted around his calves and 3:07 staring back from the dim red digits by the door. The hum had found a new register—lower, broader, a bass note that made the bed frame answer. He held the prayer stone to his chest and whispered a Psalm until the numbers turned and the room exhaled.

The next morning Ava slid into the chair across from him at breakfast like a thought he'd been avoiding. Her tray went untouched.

"It's louder," she said.

He nodded.

"It's reaching the part where they stop pretending." She lowered her voice until it was barely vibration. "When you see them, don't speak."

"Why?"

"They don't like being named." She glanced at his fist. "And they already know your name."

He opened his hand under the table. The stone was warm from his grip. A fresh nick scored one side, shallow and deliberate as a fingernail. It wasn't a crack. It was a mark. He traced it once and felt, absurdly, as if he had just underlined something he hadn't read.

He started hearing his name in daytime, a whisper threaded through ordinary sentences. "Vitals, Daniel." "Group in ten, Daniel." "Coffee's fresh, Daniel." Somewhere inside each line, a second voice harmonized. He stopped answering on the first call; it felt like talking over a hymn.

Dr. Harker noticed his hands. "You're shaking."

"I know."

"We can adjust the dose."

"I'd rather not."

"Because you're afraid of losing the signal," she said, and didn't make it a question.

He looked at the floor, ashamed and unpersuaded. "Because I'm afraid of losing the part of me that knows when the floor isn't a floor."

She nodded as if the answer had not surprised her. "Tell me if the fear gets bigger than the signal."

That night he lay on his back and counted the drips in the hallway sink he could not see. One-two-three; pause. One-two-three; pause. The hum woke early, at 3:05, exploratory, as if testing the seam. By 3:07 the lights along the baseboard winked once and gave up. Dark folded the room in half.

He could feel it before he could see it—the coolness that isn't air, the attention like the prickle of a thousand eyes behind the glass. He sat up, slow enough not to make prey-movements, and fixed his gaze on the doorway where the thin spill of the nurse's station light usually bled under the frame. The gap was a darker dark now, like a shadow cast by something with no light to block.

It was simply there. Tall, exact, a human outline drawn by someone who had never seen a face. No glow, no theatrics—just shape. It filled the space outside his door as neatly as a sentence finishing itself.

The humming stopped.

In the kind of silence that only exists after a sound has been taken away, the figure tilted its head, as if listening for the place his fear was standing. He closed his mouth on the prayer that wanted to come out, heard Ava's warning like a hand on his shoulder, and held his breath the way a swimmer holds air under ice.

It didn't move closer. It didn't need to. The tilt deepened by a fraction, like a curious bird. And in that small angle he felt recognition—not of him, but of the part of him that had drawn and drawn until the page forgot how to be blank. The part that had asked why until the question wore a groove in his mind deep enough for something else to walk in.

He pressed the stone into his palm until the edge bit. The minute refused to turn. The clock by the door, unlit now, kept its own time without telling him. He thought of Emily whispering in a kitchen that smelled like cinnamon and rain. He thought of Lily's small, serious face. He did not speak.

Somewhere down the hall, very far away, a nurse's shoes squeaked once on clean floor. The figure straightened, as if reminded of coarser physics, and the gap at the bottom of the door filled again with a thin wedge of light. When he blinked, the doorway was an ordinary doorway, innocent and empty.

The hum returned so softly he might have imagined it. He lay back and watched the ceiling until the lines settled into white. He did not sleep. The veil felt thinner than paper, and morning had an infinite distance to cross.

Chapter 12: When the Walls Tremble

Sleep no longer came in hours, or even minutes. It arrived like a mist—thin, tasteless—and vanished the instant Daniel reached for it. By the fourth night he felt hollowed out, the empty spaces inside him ringing faintly with each breath. The ward had grown colder, though the thermostat insisted on seventy-one. Even the fluorescent light along the baseboard carried a blue cast that made the skin of his forearms look unfamiliar.

Morning had the grace to pretend at normal. Trays clattered; a nurse's laugh drifted down the hall like a memory of summer. Daniel sat with his oatmeal cooling in front of him and tried to pretend with it. The spoon trembled faintly when he lifted it. Across the room, Ava watched him with her head tilted, as if he were a sound she was trying to place.

When he glanced away, the white wall to his left expanded and contracted once, gently, like the belly of a sleeping animal. He held very still and made himself count to five. The wall did not do it again.

Group therapy was a circle of chairs and soft voices, the clock's hand sweeping steadily like nothing had ever happened to time. Dr. Harker sat with her ankles crossed and her legal pad on her lap, ready but not predatory. Daniel watched mouths move and tried to match the sounds to them. Around the third admission—a man saying he'd slept eight hours for the first time in a month—voices overlapped, a double-track, the room speaking twice at different speeds. He turned to find which patient had added a second voice and saw that no one's lips were moving. For a long breath, everyone in the circle became a still image while the conversation continued above their heads.

He pinched the inside of his arm until the skin flushed and stung. The room snapped back. Harker's eyes clicked to his and held.

"Daniel?" she said, neutral as air. "With us?"

He nodded. The hum in the vents answered for him.

After group, Ava found him near the end of the hall where a mural tried to convince the wall it was a meadow. Childish wildflowers swayed on glossy paint. They didn't make the hallway warmer.

"They're thinning the veil," she said without preamble.

"How do you know?"

"I don't have to know," she said. "I can feel it. You can too."
She lifted her hand and hovered it an inch from the wall. "It's
like standing in front of a speaker. The sound is there even
when the music isn't playing."

"Who are they?" His voice came out too fast. "You keep
saying they."

Ava looked at him with something like pity. "The ones that
know your name. The ones that followed the song." She
hesitated, then added, "They've been waiting for you to see."

He wanted to argue—to say this was delusion, a shared
psychosis, a ward contagion written in whispers—but his
tongue sat heavy in his mouth, and the wall behind the
flowers breathed again, very slightly, as if in agreement.

Dr. Harker's office felt more like a confession booth than it
had before. He sat, hands open on his knees, because fists
made his forearms ache where the inked ghosts of symbols
liked to gather.

"I'm not sure I can tell what's real," he said, and hated how
easy the admission was. "But it doesn't feel like it matters. It's
happening anyway."

"What is?" Harker asked.

"The… convergence." The word embarrassed him as soon as he said it. He sounded like one of Mick's prophecies smuggled into clinical language. "The hospital and the other place. The house. The woods. I keep—They keep touching."

Harker didn't scoff. She didn't reassure, either. "How would you know if it were only in your mind?"

He looked at the window's thin rectangle of sky. "I think I'd prefer it that way."

"That's an answer," Harker said mildly, "not a test."

He waited.

Finally, she said, "You're not the first patient to describe these patterns. Or the song. Years apart, no contact with each other. Same geometry. Same… hour." A muscle in her jaw ticked. "Patterns don't equal proof, but they don't equal nonsense either."

He blinked at her. "You've seen the drawings?"

Harker looked down, and for once, he watched her choose a word. "I've... kept them."

"Why?"

"Because they repeat." She met his eyes again, a steadiness there like a handrail. "Because they scare me."

Something grateful and terrified moved under his ribs. He thought—for one rash second—of reaching across the space and catching her sleeve, just to make sure she was a person and not a skilled, articulate apparition. He kept his hands where they were.

In the afternoon, the ward soured. Metal leaked into the air again—iron pennies behind the teeth. Mick stopped long enough in his pacing to shove his sleeves up to his elbows and scratch at his forearms with the blunted ends of his fingernails until his skin went raw. "They cry 'How long?' " he muttered, breathless. "And the answer is 'Until the number is complete.' "

A nurse crouched; voice soft but firm. "Mick, stop. You're bleeding."

"Then I am counted," he said, and resumed reciting, Revelation beads slipping through his fingers, the words old enough to cut.

Sarah's pencil skittered off the page during group and clattered under the chair. She covered her ears with both hands and rocked, eyes squeezed shut. "Too loud," she choked. "They're almost here."

"What is almost here, Sarah?" a therapist asked gently.

Sarah shook her head, hair slapping her cheeks, and wouldn't open her eyes.

Back in his room, Daniel stripped off his shirt to wash his face and caught sight of himself in the small mirror above the sink. New marks ringed his left wrist like a bracelet—thin, precise, each line a tiny curve nested in another, the pattern so delicate it made his stomach drop. He rubbed at them with the rough paper towel until the skin burned and reddened. The lines remained, faintly raised, as if the skin had learned them from the inside.

At dinner, Ava noticed. She didn't ask to see, only nodded. "They're choosing you."

"For what?" It came out a whisper.

"To open." The word landed like a pebble in his throat. "Or to refuse."

He wanted to laugh at the false simplicity of that choice and could not find a laugh.

Night gathered like a planned event. Staff moved more quickly without looking like they were hurrying. Dr. Harker made two circuits of the unit that Daniel saw, speaking to nurses in low, unconcerned tones that did not match the number of times her eyes flicked to the clock.

3:03.

Sleep pretended to hover. He lay on his back and watched the seam where the ceiling met the wall. The hum came then, in the bones of the building—so deep the first sensation was nausea. His mattress gave a small, steady shiver. Somewhere, a metal cart chimed once as its frame rattled against itself.

3:06.

The light along the baseboard flickered and failed, leaving only the red line of the door's emergency indicator. It looked like a wound held closed with one careful stitch.

Daniel sat up. He didn't reach for the call button. He felt, absurdly, that to summon a person into the room would be to hand them into a place not meant for them.

3:07.

Everything in the ward seemed to remember its other name.

Alarms hiccupped awake and then fell into a tangled chorus—some shrilling, some lowing, as if every machine had been asked to sing the same song in a different key. Doors along the corridor thudded shut of their own accord, a percussion line that marched closer, paused, marched closer again. The floor vibrated under his bare feet. The hum swelled until he could feel it shining in his teeth.

Patients cried out—one, then several, then more, voices flaring and folding. Mick's baritone strained into a shout. "Behold!" he cried, and then, "Mercy," and then sobbing, which was somehow worse.

The security lights along the hall's crown guttered. For a heartbeat—long enough to write a thought on—the symbols surfaced on his wall in a pale phosphorescence, as if something beneath the paint had inhaled and pressed its ribs outward. He reached for them without meaning to, palm flattening over the cool, unyielding plaster, and the pattern fit his hand as if it had been sized to him.

He flinched and yanked back. The marks on his wrist ached, a low throb like a bruise touched again.

Past his doorway, movement gathered. Not footsteps—those he knew and could name—but displacement, like the air itself stepped sideways. He stood. The prayer stone was in his fist before memory could trace the reach.

A shape crossed the square of the open door. Not the faceless figure alone but a second shadow with it, low to the ground, jointed wrong, moving as if it remembered being something else and wanted to try that shape on. Behind them, more—less formed, more suggestion than outline, the way heat makes shapes ripple above asphalt.

The hum clipped, and in the broken edge of sound, he heard his own name, the syllables changed by distance and by something like hunger. He thought of Ava and shut his mouth fast enough to bite his tongue. The taste of iron flared.

"Daniel." Dr. Harker's voice, farther down the hall, firm as a hand catching a fall. "Everyone stays in their rooms."

Bless her, he thought wildly. Bless her voice.

Ava's door opened a crack, then wider. She stood framed in the rectangle of gloom like a figure from an icon, pale and unslept. Across the chaos, she found his eyes with the accuracy of someone aiming at a sound.

It's time, she mouthed.

Another door slammed. A nurse cursed under her breath, steady and practical. "Power's tripping—reset panel three! Panel three!"

The humming peaked, and for a moment the ward was an instrument strung too tight. Daniel felt the impulse to kneel as clearly as he had ever felt hunger. He didn't, only because his legs had turned to stone.

The lights went out.

Not flickered. Not dimmed.

Went out.

Dark laid over everything, whole and absolute, the kind of dark that erases distance and makes your own breath sound like an intruder. The alarms died mid-cry. The hum cut cleanly, leaving a quiet that rang.

In that new silence, close as breath, something exhaled. He could not have said whether it was in the hall or inside his chest.

He did not speak. He could hear his pulse like a small drum and the prayer that rose out of him without permission. Lord, keep— The sentence did not finish because there was the softest of sounds, like the pad of a child's bare foot on tile, and for the first time since he'd been brought here, he could not tell whether it came from the corridor or from just behind him in the room.

Chapter 13: The Breaking Point

The lights snapped back on as if nothing had happened, sterile fluorescents flooding the ward with their usual antiseptic glare. But nothing was the same.

The hum was gone, yes, but the air was different—thick, charged, heavy with the weight of something unseen. Every sound sharpened: the squeak of shoes down the hall, the click of a pen at the nurses' station, the nervous breathing of the patients scattered in corners and doorways.

Daniel stayed frozen, still clutching the prayer stone so tightly that the edges dug sharp crescents into his palm. He heard his own heartbeat pounding against his ribs like a warning bell, too loud in the thick silence that followed the blackout.

"Everything's fine," one of the nurses said, voice tight, rehearsed. "Power surge. We're back online."

No one believed her.

The patients whispered.

"I saw them," one muttered, rocking back and forth, eyes wide. "The ones behind the walls... I saw them this time."

"They're here," Mick said, pacing the hallway, his voice hoarse, scripture spilling out of him like blood from a wound. "They walk between the doors, and they know the hours. 'For the hour of their judgment has come.' Revelation nineteen, verse eleven. You think I don't know? I know."

Ava sat cross-legged on the far side of the common room, humming quietly to herself. She didn't look up when Daniel entered, but her humming shifted, the melody twisting slightly, almost like a warning.

Dr. Harker made her rounds in silence, calm as ever but with a new tightness in her face. She stopped at each room, speaking softly to each patient, checking vitals, offering comfort like a balm she knew wouldn't work. When she came to Daniel's door, she lingered.

"You all right?" she asked.

He wanted to answer, but his voice wouldn't work. He just nodded, throat dry, the prayer stone sweating in his hand.

Her gaze sharpened. She didn't believe the nod. "If you saw something," she said, voice quiet but firm, "I need to know."

His mouth opened, but nothing came out. How could he explain the thing standing outside his door, the way its faceless head tilted toward him like it was listening? How could he tell her that the darkness wasn't darkness at all but presence?

So he just shook his head, and her frown deepened.

By morning, the ward had changed.

Clocks glitched and froze at 3:07 every night, ticking into silence for minutes at a time before resuming like nothing had happened. Journals and Bibles—some patients' and even one belonging to a nurse—were found torn apart in empty rooms, pages scattered in messy circles across the floor. Doors that should have been locked in the night were left open, the sensors tripped, but the security footage only showed static during the hours they were opened.

And Daniel... Daniel was losing time again.

He woke one morning with ink under his nails and the smell of marker clinging to his fingers. His walls were covered in symbols—layer upon layer of circles, spirals, and runes. Some he recognized from Lily's drawings. Others felt new, foreign, yet disturbingly familiar. The marks on his wrists burned, raw and raised as though the lines had been carved into his skin.

When Dr. Harker asked him in their session if he had been drawing at night, his mouth said no before his mind could even think of the truth.

"Daniel," she said softly, watching him closely, "you're not the only one who's... seeing things. These patterns—they repeat. Across patients. Across years. But no one's ever been able to tell me what they mean."

"You've seen this before," he said, leaning forward, voice sharp.

Her eyes flickered, just for a moment, and for the first time, Daniel saw fear in them.

Later, Ava found him in the dayroom.

"They've chosen you," she said quietly, her pale fingers tracing the lines on his wrist as if memorizing them. "It's your voice they've been waiting for."

Daniel swallowed hard. "What do they want from me?"

Her gaze lifted to his, steady and unblinking. "Don't let them speak through you," she whispered. "If you do... you won't come back."

That night, the hum began earlier—closer to two-thirty.

It started soft, just a tremor in the floor, but by the time the red glow of the clock bled into the numbers 3:00, it was vibrating the walls, making the bed frame hum like a struck string. The smell of damp earth and rot seeped in, thick and cloying, coating the back of his throat until he wanted to retch.

Patients screamed down the hall. Some prayed, frantic whispers that broke into sobs. Others laughed—high, manic laughter that cut off as suddenly as it started.

Daniel pressed himself into the corner of the room, clutching the stone, heart hammering so hard it hurt.

At 3:07, the humming stopped.

The silence that followed was worse.

Slowly, the figure appeared in the doorway. No flicker this time, no blink-and-miss—it was there, solid and still, a shadow wearing the shape of a man, faceless but aware. The air around it buzzed, an electric charge crawling over his skin.

It stepped inside.

One step. Then another.

The hum roared back to life inside Daniel's skull, deafening, suffocating, vibrating through his teeth, through the stone in his hand, through the floor itself. He pressed himself harder into the wall, shaking his head, whispering, "No, no, no—"

The figure tilted its head, just like before.

And then, soft as breath, Ava's voice from the doorway:

"It's almost here."

The lights died again.

Darkness swallowed the room.

Chapter 14: The Descent

The darkness didn't just fill the room—it devoured it.

It was not the kind of dark you meet when the lights go out. This was heavier, tactile, a black that clung like wet fabric and pressed into his pores. It stole even the whisper of the vents. Daniel's breath rasped in his throat, too loud, too human, so he clamped a hand over his mouth, terrified they could hear it. His lungs burned from the effort of being silent.

Then the hum came back.

Not the familiar vibration he had grown used to in the ward—the muted, mechanical sigh of old ducts and humming fluorescents. This hum was deeper, monstrous, layered with whispers that weren't whispers at all. Ancient syllables cracked and reformed, like teeth grinding against each other inside his skull. They crawled under his skin, threading into his nerves until his muscles twitched in rhythm with the sound.

And cutting through that awful chorus, sweet as a scalpel dipped in honey, came one voice:

Daddy…

Daniel's head snapped toward the doorway, though there was nothing but liquid dark. The voice was unmistakable. Lily— gentle, lilting, calling the way she had when she wanted one more story before bed. His knees shook.

"Lily?" His voice was hoarse, barely a thread.

The air shifted instantly. Cold slashed down his throat with every breath, sharp enough to sting his lungs. The hum pulsed through the tile beneath his bare feet, steady as the beat of some massive, hidden heart just below the floor.

Across the hall, something scraped—slow, deliberate. A chair dragged across tile by invisible hands, the screech echoing like a blade across steel. Then a door began to rattle violently, slamming again and again in an erratic rhythm before halting mid-slam, the silence louder than the noise.

Daniel pressed the prayer stone into his palm until it bit skin. He felt it break him open—heat, pressure, blood. And now the smell rose too: not just the rot of damp earth and leaves, but copper—iron—blood thick enough to sting the back of his throat.

A sharp crack! split the air. The clock had fallen from the wall. Its glass face shattered across the floor, but the hands were frozen at 3:07. No twitch. No mercy.

Screams erupted down the hall.

High, raw, animal sounds, as if people had been stripped of words and left with nothing but noise. Above them all came laughter—a man's laughter, wild and endless, until it broke into gasps and sobs. Sarah's voice cut through sharp as broken glass:

"They're pulling us through! They're pulling us through!"

Mick dropped to his knees in the common room, rocking so hard the floor shuddered under his weight. His voice, ragged, tried to summon scripture:

"And I saw heaven opened... behold a white horse... His name is Faithful and True—"

But the words collapsed into sobs, spit and blood flying from his bitten lip as he whispered the same mangled line again and again.

Staff scrambled with flashlights, but the beams dimmed mid-stride, as if the dark itself drank batteries. Shadows bled across the floor like liquid. The smell of bleach, sweat, and fear thickened into something metallic and sour.

Then—a hand seized Daniel's wrist.

It was cold, trembling, but real. Human.

Ava.

Her pupils were blown wide, swallowing the light, but her voice was steady, knife-sharp. "They want to wear you," she whispered, dragging him close, her nails cutting crescents into his arm. "That's what the marks are. A door. Don't speak to them, Daniel. Don't let them in."

"What are they?" His voice cracked. His jaw trembled with it.

Her whisper shredded into ragged breath. "Old. Older than words. And they've been waiting for you to listen."

The air split.

Reality fractured with a hum so violent his teeth rattled. The darkness flickered like a dying bulb, the ward vanishing in a strobe—and in its place, the clearing from Old Rag. The stone circle blazed with pale, impossible light, symbols writhing across its face like things alive.

And Lily stood barefoot in the center.

Her nightgown clung to her legs as if soaked. Bun-Bun dangled from one hand. Her lips moved in a chant he couldn't hear over the roar. The sight of her froze him—his whole body vibrating with the rising hum. His bones ached with it; his jaw locked against the pressure.

Then her eyes darkened, swallowed whole by the void he had seen before. She raised her hand and pointed behind him.

He turned.

Dr. Harker's flashlight slashed the dark, hot white across his face.

"Daniel!" Her voice was iron, commanding, steady enough to slice the roar. "Stay with me. Stay here."

Her grip latched onto his arm, sharp and anchoring. She dragged him backward, her breath fast but measured, her presence the only sane gravity in the room. She shoved him into his room and slammed the door, the lock clicking hard from the outside.

"Stay inside. No matter what you hear. Do not open this door."

The flashlight beam vanished. Her footsteps were devoured by the roar.

Minutes—hours—time collapsed. The dark pressed closer, vibrating with voices that shifted and merged into a horrible, layered hymn.

Then came the first voice—sharp, intimate, slicing the din.

"Daniel." Emily's voice. Warm. Familiar. "It's me. Open the door. Please, honey, I need you. You know my voice."

His chest locked. He pressed his back against the wall, fists shaking around the stone.

Then another voice—low, smooth, sliding into his ear like oil.

100

"I can give them back to you. Both of them. Emily. Lily. The life you had. Just say yes."

The prayer stone burned hotter and hotter in his palm until he dropped it. It hit tile and cracked in two, the sound impossibly loud in the suffocating dark.

The hum surged into a roar, his name chanted by dozens of voices, warped, twisted, overlapping like hooks tearing through his chest.

He almost answered. His lips formed the shape of Lily's name. His heart lurched to open. The door handle trembled under his gaze, just inches from his shaking hand.

"Amen!" Ava's voice cut through from somewhere beyond the walls, urgent, desperate, serrated. "Don't answer them, Daniel! No matter what you hear!"

He collapsed against the bedframe, teeth clenched until his jaw screamed. The roar buckled, broke—and the world tilted sideways, plunging him into nothing but black.

Chapter 15: Clues and Allies

Morning came like a mercy that didn't quite believe in itself.
A pale bar of light seeped through the slit of Daniel's window
and laid itself across the floor as if testing whether this room
could still hold day. He woke on top of the covers, jaw aching
from how hard he'd clenched it, every muscle sore the way a
body feels after bracing all night against a storm.

His prayer stone lay cracked on the tile where he'd dropped
it. Two pieces, jagged as broken teeth. When he picked them
up, warmth pulsed through both halves as if the heat had
been trapped inside and never cooled. He held them together
and felt the seam find itself—imperfect, but aligning. He
slipped both pieces into his pocket, an anchor in duplicate.

The ward was quieter than quiet—subdued without the calm.
Patients moved as if gravity had been turned up a notch. Staff
spoke in low, professional voices that tried not to use words
like last night or blackout. Someone had righted the fallen
clock and rehung it. It ticked, obedient, as if nothing
important had ever happened at 3:07 in the morning.

Ava sat alone in the common room at a table by the window,
a pencil working furiously over cheap paper. The angle of her
shoulder said she expected to be interrupted and meant to
finish anyway. Daniel approached slowly, palms open on the

table before he sat, so she could see he wasn't bringing more fear than she already carried.

"What are you drawing?" he asked, voice rough.

She didn't look up. "Not mine," she said. "I don't choose them." The pencil paused and cut a sure curve. "They show me things. I just… keep the record."

He watched lines become circles, circles become a pattern with ribs, as if a skeleton were assembling itself. The shape wasn't one he recognized outright, and yet a pressure behind his eyes told him he'd seen it—if not here, then in the negative space of another drawing, in the gap between two notes of Lily's humming. He reached without meaning to, then stopped himself. "I know this," he said softly.

Ava's mouth curled, not into a smile exactly but into the idea of one. "Of course you do," she said. "It knows you back."

He swallowed. "Ava… last night—"

"I know." She finally met his eyes. "I'm still here too."

Footsteps approached. Daniel looked up to see Dr. Harker standing in the doorway, a posture of unflappable. She nodded once to him, once to Ava, and crooked a finger just enough to be invitation rather than order.

"Daniel," she said when they were in her office, "you have a visitor in twenty minutes—if you want one." She glanced at the file in her hand. "Father Grayson. Your wife asked if—" Harker stopped herself, recalibrating. "She thought it might comfort you."

For the first time in days, something like breath moved freely in Daniel's chest. "Yes," he said, faster than caution. "Please."

Harker's gaze softened by a fraction. "All right. It will be supervised, as required. I'll stay out of the way as much as I can." She hesitated, then added, "He sounded... steady."

He nodded, unwilling to trust his voice around gratitude.

They met in a small visiting room that had pretended to be a family lounge—two chairs, a table with old magazines, a window on a piece of sky that could have been painted there. Father Grayson walked in with his Bible tucked under his arm and the kind of tired that looks like it's been prayed into a tool, not a wound.

"Daniel." He said the name as if he were returning it.

Something in Daniel gave way. He stood too quickly, the chair legs screeching. "I can't—" he began, and words collided in his mouth—humming, voices, Lily—and broke apart. He swallowed the shards. "I don't know how to fight something I can't name," he said finally. "And it knows my name."

Grayson crossed the room and gripped his shoulders, not to restrain, just to confirm mass. "You're not alone," he said simply. "You're not abandoned." He opened the Bible not like a prop but like a door he'd used before. "You don't have to make the right words. You just have to be willing to be held."

They prayed. Not performative, not loud. A few lines, steady as heartbeat, a request stitched to a confession, stitched to a promise not authored by either of them. As they spoke, the pressure in the room eased—not gone, not defeated, but as if something listening took three steps back to consider.

For the first time in nights, the hum receded so far Daniel could not hear it. He became aware of smaller sounds: the page whisper as Grayson closed the Bible; the sigh of air through the vent; his own breath, which did not sound like a man drowning.

"Emily told me about the symbols," Grayson said after a moment, like a man approaching a skittish animal. "What you've seen. What Lily drew."

Daniel nodded. "You think I'm sick," he said, testing the possible betrayals in the statement.

"I think you are suffering," Grayson said, voice low. "And I think the boundary between suffering and mystery is thin enough to bruise. I also think the ground under this building remembers more than the administration does."

Daniel looked up.

"It used to be church land," Grayson continued. "Parish maps from the twenties call it a mission tract. There was a chapel here—small, stone, probably little more than four walls and a bell. Torn down when they built the first wing." He shrugged. "Or so the papers say."

Harker's earlier admission found purchase in that. Patterns. Hours. Kept drawings. "A chapel," Daniel repeated, the word ringing. "Ava told me she's seen a room with walls that hum. She called it a chapel."

Grayson's eyebrows lifted. "Then we're speaking of the same thing."

"Do you know where?" Daniel asked.

"No," Grayson admitted. "But if it was left standing—or left underneath—then it would be... below."

Below. The stairwells. The way the hum thickened near the service corridor. Daniel felt it like a compass needle stutter toward north.

On the way back to the unit, the world resumed its mercies and its threats. A nurse passed with a plastic bin of little paper cups. An orderly laughed at something on his phone and cut the sound when he saw Daniel and Father Grayson. A door at the end of the hall was marked STAFF ONLY in a font that wanted to be obeyed more than it wanted to be read.

Later, after Grayson had gone with a promise to return and a touch to Daniel's shoulder that didn't pretend to heal what it couldn't, Daniel wandered close to that door. Not touching. Just... listening.

The air changed. Not colder. Denser. He could feel the hum there like a cat feels thunder before weather admits it. He took a half-step closer.

"Mr. Cross." The nurse's voice was polite and absolute. Daniel turned to find a woman in scrubs, her badge swaying on its clip. He recognized her—Marisol, nights and early mornings, meticulous with meds, kind without being soft. "That wing is for staff," she said, a gentleness wrapping the hard edge. "Let's head back toward the dayroom."

He nodded, let himself be steered, and did not say thank you for pretending this is about rules. As they walked, he glanced back. The door looked back, innocuous as a closet.

Ava slid into the chair across from him at dinner as if she'd grown out of the air. She laid a folded sheet of paper on the table between them and pressed two fingers to it—do not turn it yet. Her eyes flicked to the nurses' station, then back.

"They were louder near the stairwell," she said casually, as if discussing the weather. "Last night. Before everything went... wrong."

He kept his hands still. "You were out of your room."

Her mouth twitched. "So were you."

"Is that—" He tipped his chin at the paper. "—a drawing you chose?"

"I don't choose them," she reminded him. "This one came with a direction."

He unfolded the paper under the table with careful hands. The lines weren't symbols this time so much as architecture—a schematic rendered by impression instead of measure. Rectangles for rooms, a run of squares for steps, a hall that bent at a wrong angle, then straightened. Along one wall, she'd drawn small marks that weren't letters but carried the feeling of words. At the end: a box shaded darker, with a circle inside it and lines radiating outward like a silent bell.

"How do you know this is… real?" he asked, even as his body leaned toward believing.

Ava tilted her head. "They don't usually waste my time." She touched the page, her finger resting on the bell. "They don't want you down there."

"Which," he said, hearing how tired courage can sound like arrogance, "means that's where the answers are."

She held his gaze a heartbeat, then nodded once. "Bring your stone," she said. "Both pieces."

The rest of the day arranged itself into the shape of waiting. Group was a low murmur about breathing exercises. A tech replaced a flickering ballast with a practiced reach and an indifferent whistle. Mick dozed with his Bible open on his chest, lips still moving the way a man's do when prayer has switched from words to pulse. Sarah drew nothing and stared at everything.

Harker caught Daniel on the way back from the bathroom, not to scold, not to pry—just to calibrate. "How are you now?" she asked.

"Less broken," he said before his defenses could draft an answer. "Not fixed."

Her mouth quirked. "That's a category I recognize." She glanced toward the unit doors and lowered her voice. "I allowed Father Grayson up because your wife asked, yes. But also because sometimes the right visitor adjusts the weight in a room." A pause, then: "If you feel the weight shift toward danger, come to me first. Not after."

He nodded. "If I feel the weight shift toward answers?"

"That's usually the same thing," she said dryly, and let him go.

Evening smoothed the ward's loud edges. Dinner trays rattled and vanished. Meds came and went. The baseboard lights glowed with a color that tried to pass for warm. Somewhere a nurse told a story in Spanish and ended it with a laugh that lifted, genuine and brief.

Daniel sat at the window and watched a smeared sunset consider becoming night. He took the two halves of his prayer stone from his pocket. They lay in his palm like a broken coin. He pressed the seam together. Heat gathered where the edges met, a faint, persistent throb, not painful—alive. He whispered, "Lord, keep," and couldn't decide which word should come next—me, her, us, them—so he left the prayer raw and unfinished on purpose, an opening no thing with teeth could use.

Across the room, Ava hummed under her breath, the melody so like Lily's bedtime song that for one tight second he could see his daughter's small hand patting the space beside her on the blanket—here, Daddy; here.

The ward held its breath, but not with menace, not yet. More like an animal at the edge of water, scenting rain. The quiet was not peace. It was a pause with muscles in it.

Night would come, and with it, the hour that pretended to be an hour and was really a wound. Between now and then, there was the door marked STAFF ONLY, a set of stairs that didn't go where the architect had intended, and a room Ava called a chapel where walls remembered how to hum.

Daniel slid the stone halves back into his pocket, stood, and tested his balance against the floor. He felt the hospital under him and, somewhere under that, a bell no one had rung in a very long time.

"Soon," Ava said without looking up from her page.

He nodded, to her and to the weight of the coming, and to the faint, stubborn mercy of a day that had not broken him. Not yet.

Chapter 16: The Forbidden Wing

The hum woke in the bones of the building before dawn, a bass line no one had asked for. It moved through conduits and metal studs, pressed up from the concrete like water through a bad foundation. Daniel felt it in the seam of the stone halves in his pocket, a faint, repeating throb that wasn't his pulse.

He found Ava already watching the STAFF ONLY door from the corner chair where she'd been pretending to sleep. She didn't look at him when he stopped beside her; she just tipped her head toward the door, listening as if it were a throat clearing before a speech.

"It's time to see," she said.

He almost smiled at the simplicity of it. "They want me alone."

"That's why I'm coming," she said, finally meeting his eyes. "Two is harder to wear."

Footsteps approached from the far end of the hall— measured, unhurried. Father Grayson came into view with his hands in the pockets of a tired coat, the collar bent a little from the way his fingers had gripped it in the cold. He gave them each a nod that held more than greeting.

"Couldn't sleep," he said, and then, lower: "You're not going down there without a prayer."

Ava's mouth twitched. "Faith cuts both ways down there," she warned.

"Everything sharp does," Grayson said. "But I'd rather bring a sword than my hands."

The ward's attention shifted in their favor when a crash rang from the dayroom—the metallic tumble of a tray cart, a patient's startled shout, staff voices rising. For a brief slice of time, eyes and cameras looked the other way. Daniel moved first. The STAFF ONLY door pushed open beneath his palm with the reluctant give of a thing accustomed to being obeyed.

The stairwell air was colder. Older, somehow. It smelled of wet stone and a sweetness that might have been old incense or the memory of it. The hum grew stronger with each step, flickers of light jittering down the concrete walls in syncopation with their footfalls.

"Listen," Ava said softly, halfway down. "Do you hear it changing?"

He did. The tone layered—one note under another, like a harmony being added. He couldn't tell if the harmony was meant to comfort or to mimic comfort badly enough to hurt.

They reached a landing with a locked fire door. A sign announced MAINTENANCE SUBLEVEL in a font that thought rules kept their own promises. The handle didn't budge for Daniel; it did for Grayson, who took a breath first as if he were about to enter someone's bedroom uninvited and wanted to get the apology right.

Beyond, the hallway narrowed. Pipes ran the ceiling. The lights were older here, their casings yellowed, their hum answering the hum in the walls the way a tuning fork answers its twin. On the left: a long storage cage, rust bit into its wire. On the right: a closed door painted the kind of gray hospitals use when they don't want anyone to notice the door is there.

Ava's fingers brushed Daniel's sleeve, not a grab, a gauge. "Left," she murmured.

He frowned toward the cage. "Storage?"

"Not the cage," she said. "Behind it."

They followed the aisle to the end, where mops and buckets
died. The wire panel there had a padlock, new and
disappointed in the old metal it had been asked to secure. The
padlock was not their problem. The cage didn't meet the wall
by an inch; someone had installed it on a hurry day. Ava slid
her hand through the gap and found the latch meant to be
out of reach. The wire groaned. Grayson set his shoulder, and
together they dragged the corner enough to let Daniel slip
behind.

Back there, light thinned. Dust hung as if waiting to be
named. The wall was block and then, suddenly, not block: a
rectangle the color of shut mouths, paint slightly smoother
than the wall around it. A seam. No knob. A place where a
door had been persuaded to forget it was a door. He laid his
palm flat. The hum answered from the other side like
recognition.

"It's here," he said.

Grayson came around the cage with a grunt, dust in his hair.
He looked at the wall, then at Daniel, then upward as if
orientation might come from above. "Lord have mercy," he
said, which could have been a prayer or a diagnosis.

"How do we open it?" Daniel asked, even as the stone halves in his pocket began to warm, the sensation gathering at the edges like a bruise flushing under a thumb.

Ava pulled the folded paper from her sleeve—the map she'd given Daniel and he'd memorized and distrusted in equal measure. She turned it sideways and set it against the wall, aligning her pencil marks with hairline irregularities in the paint until her breath steadied. "Here," she said, tapping four spots in a pattern. "Knock. Slow. Then hold the last one."

Daniel looked at Grayson, who looked back with a shrug that said we have done stranger things together and alone. Daniel knocked. One. Two. Three. On the fourth he kept his palm there. Heat built under his hand—not sharp, not burning, just a pressure asking politely to be admitted.

Something under the paint sighed. Metal unlatched without sound. The rectangle shivered and then tipped inward by a quarter inch, enough to catch, enough to insist.

They went in.

The corridor beyond felt narrower because the walls remembered when they had been trees. Moisture beaded along a conduit. Their breaths made small ghosts in front of their faces. On the right, a utility room with shelves of old logbooks and clipboards gone soft at the corners. On the left, a door with a small wired-glass window, the glass fogged from within as if the room breathed.

"Here," Ava said again, softer now, more a tone than a word.

They stepped into the utility room, because even in hauntings paper has a way of asserting itself. Daniel picked up the top log, the leather cracking like dried bark. The ink had bled. Still, dates marched their narrow lines: 1911, 1912, 1917. The handwriting was careful, the way people used to write when they knew the world would judge them for sloppiness even if it had to lean close to do it.

Patient episodes coincide with evening prayers.

Woke the ward at three and seven past. Hymns unsettled— the humming heard through stone.

Seal mentioned by Father Álvarez. Admonition: stop counting things God sealed. Counter-admonition: learn the lock if the house is full of wind.

The words thinned into mold here and there, then thickened again. Daniel flipped further. Antechamber below chapel holds sound. Do not pray there without fasting. Symbols

118

match those seen by child in bed six. The page stung his finger with a paper cut, as if to prove itself real.

Grayson had found a thin ledger with a priest's hand— Spanish curling into English now and then, the sentences like someone walking between languages without caring who saw. " 'This ground is thin,' " he read, not for the first time a man reading something to himself out loud because he could not bear to have it only in his head. " 'Prayers are heard but not always answered by the one to whom they are addressed.' " His mouth tightened. "And then here: 'A door is not a blessing just because it opens.' "

They moved on. The door with the wired-glass window looked into a closet of relics that had wanted to be forgotten: a brass handbell slick with tarnish; a box of cracked white candles; a small wooden cross with one arm burned dark, as if someone had tried to cauterize a wound in it. Ava's gaze snagged on the bell and didn't let go.

"It's the same," she said. "From the drawing."

"We don't take it," Grayson said gently, as if talking to a child and to himself. "We're not here to strip a body."

At the corridor's end: another door. Wood this time, ancient and stubborn. Carved in its face—faint, shallow—the lines of circles and eyes the way stone remembers hands. Daniel reached for the handle and stopped when the hum shifted to something like breath held. He looked at the others. Grayson nodded once. Ava's chin dipped. The handle turned like a vow.

The chapel had been small when people were inside it; without them, it felt bigger. The air held a cold with a mind in it. Pews slouched in two rows, their wood eating itself. Against the far wall, a low stone altar cracked through the middle like Daniel's prayer stone. The crack ran front to back, a straight dark seam, as if the thing had decided to share the wound with anyone who came to look.

The walls had been painted once. Time had sucked most of the color out, but the shapes remained—the symbols Daniel had drawn until his knuckles hurt, layered and layered until paint became a palimpsest of intention. They were faded to the color of dried blood. They did not pulse. But standing there made Daniel's heart walk out of step with itself.

Grayson stayed by the door at first, the way you do when you are not sure if you are welcome. He bowed his head, not quite closing his eyes. Ava drifted to the left wall and lifted her hand but did not touch it.

Daniel approached the altar because not approaching it would have been a lie. The seam down the center made a line that wanted filling. His fingers hovered over it and then descended as if obeying something more honest than caution. The stone was not cold. It was the temperature of skin no longer afraid of winter.

When he touched the seam, the hum didn't rise. It reversed— like a tide drawing back from shore so far that you can see the shape of the sea floor and realize how little water had covered you to begin with.

He wasn't in the chapel.

He was in the clearing below Old Rag, the circle bright enough to live behind his eyes after he'd shut them. The trees stood attentive as witnesses. The hospital's white angles stitched through the trunks the way a dream steals from a day and expects not to be noticed. Lily stood at the edge of the circle, Bun-Bun under her arm, the rabbit's remaining eye catching a moon that wasn't anywhere Daniel knew. Tears streaked her cheeks, not loud ones—straight, serious tracks.

"Bug," he said, and the word didn't echo because the air wanted to keep it.

She shook her head once, a small refusal. When she spoke, the sound came like a word pressed through two rooms. "They won't stop until you finish what was started."

"What did I start?" he asked, and hated the truth that stood up in his mouth: What did they start in me that I let grow?

She looked past him, to the circle, to the place the faceless figure liked to stand. "The song," she said, and her mouth said Daddy at the same time her eyes said goodbye.

He snapped back into the chapel so hard he had to grab the altar to keep from falling. His chest hurt. The seam in the stone felt hot under his palm, as if the touch had an echo.

Grayson's hand was on his shoulder before Daniel could pull a breath. "With me," the priest said quietly. "You're here."

Ava's face had gone paler than usual but steadier. "They know we've found it," she said. "They know where the stitched place is thin."

The hum returned—no longer tide, more weather coming over the ridge. Doors in the corridor banged in sequence like a polite person knocking harder. Somewhere a pipe sang. The overhead light in the chapel flickered once, twice, and steadied so dimly it made everything look farther away.

"Take nothing," Grayson said. "Mark nothing. We come as witnesses."

Daniel nodded, though his palm wanted to pry at the seam and his pocket wanted to give up the stone. Ava turned and took one last look at the bell in the reliquary's window. She murmured something that might have been a word and might have been the sound a person makes when they stop themselves.

They stepped back into the hall. The hum followed, pleased with itself. It felt behind them like breath on the neck. Halfway to the stairwell, the door they had first slipped through clanged shut of its own accord; a second later, the padlock on the cage thunked against the wire as if struck from inside.

"They're herding us," Ava said.

"Then we go where we planned," Grayson returned. "Haste without hurry."

They moved faster. The lights along the ceiling guttered into a staccato that turned the hall into a strip of old film. In the strobes, Daniel saw the suggestion of a figure at the corridor's far bend—there, not there; tall, exact. He refused to run. Running cedes ground you might need later.

At the stairwell, the air hit warmer. The hum pressed once more, a firm hand between Daniel's shoulder blades, and let them go, as if granting them a head start for sport. The door to the ward gave way under Grayson's shove, and sound flooded them—ordinary sound, miraculous for its smallness: nurses talking, a TV murmuring news no one watched, the squeak of wheels that wanted oil.

They did not stop moving until they were three doors past the STAFF ONLY sign and the ward had wrapped them in its fluorescent insistence that everything be simple.

Ava slid into her chair like a person who'd just walked out of weather. Grayson pressed his hand flat on the nearest wall and whispered a sentence Daniel didn't catch. Daniel leaned against the window and let his body learn that it was allowed to shake.

"Answers," he said to no one. "We found some."

"Found a place to ask better questions," Grayson corrected gently.

Ava closed her eyes. "And we're seen now. Truly seen."

The hum, back to its upstairs pitch, purred through the baseboards like a patient cat. Not louder. Closer. As if something that had been listening from a distance all this time had finally decided the game could move into the room.

Above them, day groped for the edges of the sky. On the ward, a nurse laughed at a joke and shushed herself. In his pocket, the broken stone halves warmed together, the seam aligning and drifting apart with each breath like a wound learning and unlearning how to close.

Chapter 17: Night Terrors

By afternoon the ward remembered how to pretend. Trays clattered, a TV murmured weather, and someone laughed at a joke too small to carry. Yet under everything lay the same taut wire: the hum, thinner now but constant, like a note a violinist holds to keep the room in tune with fear. Daniel could feel it when he leaned against the wall, an almost-sound that made his fillings ache.

Ava sat angled toward the window, sketching as if her hand belonged to someone else. Father Grayson lingered at the threshold, talking with a nurse in tones that said nothing while saying I am not leaving. Dr. Harker walked the unit with a steady pace and a new way of looking at corners, like a person who has learned the house has more rooms than the realtor mentioned.

Small things misbehaved. The microwave clock in the kitchenette leapt forward two minutes, then slid back. A Bible on the dayroom shelf lay open to Psalms and then, an hour later, to Revelation, though no one had touched it. A patient's photo of a dog—tacked to a corkboard with two pins— shifted to the left by the width of a thumbnail. Staff noticed and did what people do when noticing won't help: they straightened the picture, shut the Bible, tapped the microwave, and told their shoulders to drop.

"Daniel." Harker's voice from the doorway of her office, not quite a summons. He followed her in and sat. The window made a pale rectangle behind her. She didn't pick up a pen.

"What did you find down there?" she asked.

He told her what he could without telling her he had touched an altar and woken up in a forest stitched to a hospital. The corridor. The logs. The priest's handwriting. The chapel cracked down the center like a prayer stone.

Harker listened until the story placed them both at the foot of stairs neither wanted to climb again. "During the expansion," she said, voice carefully flat, "contractors reported... interference. Tools moved. Batteries drained. A man quit midshift and told me the basement sings. I wrote it down and filed it under contactor attrition because I didn't know where else to put it."

"You believe me," he said before he could stop himself.

"I believe something is happening," she said. "I believe you are perceiving it, and I no longer find the word only useful when placed in front of perceiving." A beat. "And I believe this building has a memory."

He let out a breath that sounded like relief until he heard it. "Then we're not crazy."

"I didn't say that," she returned, dry, and then softened. "But we are not alone in it."

Clouds shouldered in around evening, the sky darkening from the edges as if a lid were lowering. The first slap of rain against the long hall windows sounded like someone scattering a fistful of gravel. A nurse announced a storm advisory none of them needed. The intercom clicked and delivered its low, calm instructions: lock interior doors; keep nonessential electronics off; minimize movement between units.

The storm obliged with immediacy. Wind shouldered the building. Lightning stitched a white seam along the floor under the doors and went quiet. The emergency lights sighed into dim red. Phones died without ceremony. The hum climbed, not in volume but in presence, as if it had been given a stage.

When the power hiccuped for real, the ward slid into a kind of lit dusk. Daniel felt the hair on his arms rise. "Lockdown," someone muttered, and the doors obeyed.

It started like a wave you'd see only from above: one cry, then three, then the whole unit speaking at once in different tones. A man's scream sharpened and held. A woman laughed and jammed her knuckles in her mouth to stop. Daniel turned and saw motion at the edges of light—long, deliberate—like a person taking a step from behind a curtain and reconsidering. Every time he tried to look directly, the shape dissolved, leaving the sense of having been seen.

Ava slid off her chair mid-breath, not fainting—leaving. She hit the floor on her knees, eyes open but not here, pencil already in her hand. Paper tore across her lap as her wrist flew. The graphite sang. Circles nested in circles, bars and ribs aligning into a geometry Daniel recognized without wanting to: not the seals he had drawn, but ones he hadn't, not yet, as if her hand had skipped time and returned with copies.

"Stay with me," Harker called, voice pitched to cut chaos without adding to it. "You're safe. Breathe." The words landed where they could. A tech moved from patient to patient, counting, anchoring with the touch of a hand on a shoulder. Father Grayson stood in the center of the ward and prayed the way men square their stance in wind: nothing performative, nothing theatrical. "Lord, be near," he said. "Lord, stay the hand. Lord, keep."

The hum took the words and did not return them. It threaded the beds, the ceiling panels, the metal frames of chairs, adding vibration to everything that thought itself still. Daniel gripped the rail at the foot of his bed and felt it sing like a struck tuning fork.

The clocks all found 3:07 and waited there.

He knew before it happened. The air told him. He felt his chest adjust to accommodate a blow. The hum swelled—no longer under, no longer around, but through—until the room was merely the water it carried. Lightning unseamed the sky and stitched it shut again. The building shook from some depth that had nothing to do with wind.

Daniel was in the clearing. The forest lined itself as witnesses. The circle burned with a low, merciless light. Lily stood inside it, Bun-Bun crooked like always, small chin lifted the way she did when a doctor asked a question she intended to answer truthfully.

"It's breaking, Daddy," she said, and her voice was too clear to be a dream's. "You can't stop it now."

"What is breaking? My mind?" He hated the plea in it, how it made him the boy he had been in foster kitchens, asking if the next house would keep him.

She swallowed and her eyes went dark-not-empty again, covered by that hand of void he'd learned to recognize. "The next thing," she said softly, which could have been mercy or prophecy, and the circle brightened until the trees leaned back from it like heat.

A crack tore the clearing. Not a sound—a severing, as if the ground had decided to become two grounds and was making the case with force. Daniel's teeth stung. The light collapsed and he was in his body, his hands cold on the bedrail, his breath loud. Somewhere, a man wailed the way a building might if it realized suddenly that all its doors opened onto the same room.

"Count!" Harker shouted to staff, voice low and slicing. "Count!"

Numbers rose and fell. Doors opened—three inches, then six, then closed—because this ward had learned not to throw anything wide too quickly. A nurse called a room number. "Empty." Another called, "Bed unoccupied." A third voice broke on, "She was here; I tucked her in."

Father Grayson crossed himself, not as show, but because some old muscle had remembered what a hand can ward. "Mercy," he breathed, and made the word sound like a door stood in.

Daniel moved without realizing he was moving. Ava's papers were everywhere, the seals he had not drawn yet duplicated ten times in a stuttered cascade. One page was different: the circle he knew, unadorned, like a hole punched in the light. In the center a small oval like an eye and, inside it, a dot. The dot felt like being named.

"Ava." He crouched by her. "Ava, come back."

Her hand stilled. The pencil fell, rolled, stopped against his shoe. She blinked hard, and the ward climbed back into her. "Second," she whispered, voice sanded down. "The second broke. Did you hear it?"

"I heard it," he said, and tasted copper as if a thought had cut his mouth.

Harker knelt with a chart she wasn't reading, her breath even only because she was making it that way. "How many?"

A nurse answered. "Three rooms empty. No signs of exit. Doors locked. Cameras—" She broke off. "Static."

"Three," Grayson repeated, as though numbers sometimes need a priest. "We speak their names." He did, careful and whole, each name given the dignity of a pause. When he finished, the ward felt larger, the way a house feels after a move-out: more space, more echo, more chances for a person to feel small.

The storm shoved the windows again. The red emergency lights licked the walls in a slow pulse. In that animal glow, Daniel saw the faintest suggestion on the tile by one of the empty beds—a dark tracery that didn't glisten like water. He stepped closer. A symbol had scorched itself into the floor: a circle braided into another with a small crossbar where they touched. If he shut his eyes he could believe heat still lived in it.

Harker saw it too. The skin around her mouth tightened. "We secure the rooms," she said. "We document." Her hands moved more quietly than her words. She looked up at Daniel. "You do not go anywhere alone tonight."

He nodded, because he had no desire to argue with wisdom when the floor itself had started learning new languages.

Ava slid into the chair nearest him, pale as paper, breathing like someone who had just run and couldn't remember why. "They're not waiting anymore," she said.

"Waiting for what?" Daniel asked, not expecting a kindness.

"For permission." She rubbed her wrist where the marks had risen in a thin bracelet. "For you."

Lightning flared again, and the unit's power dipped all the way to whispering, then steadied in that dim insistence that had begun to feel like the new day. The wind stepped back. The rain recalibrated to a steadier, colder fall. Somewhere someone sobbed into a pillow and someone else laughed because sobbing would have carried him away.

Daniel pressed the halves of the prayer stone together in his pocket until heat gathered around the seam. "Lord," he said under the noise, "keep." He couldn't bring himself to add them or me or her, not because he feared choosing wrong, but because he felt the word might be greedy under the circumstances.

Harker moved through the ward counting again, as if numbers could pet the fur of something bristled. Grayson sat, finally, on a worn chair and put his face in his hands, praying in a rumble that made the air gentler where it passed. The clock over the nurses' station blinked back to life, considered its options, and chose 3:12 as if that would help.

Ava lifted her head and looked at Daniel like people do when they deliver news they wish were not theirs to give. Her voice had the steadiness of a person stating weather.

134

"The second seal is broken," she said. "And they're not waiting anymore."

Chapter 18: The Forbidden Pulse

Morning put its face to the glass and didn't come inside.

The storm had moved off, but the ward felt like a room someone had just left: chairs slightly askew, air warm with breath that wasn't there anymore. Staff moved with the slow precision of people who had decided not to look at the clock if it meant looking at what the clock had said at 3:07. Patients spoke in pocketed whispers, as if words might set something back in motion.

The hum had changed. It wasn't gnawing at the walls or pecking at the lights. It had settled into a rhythm, steady and low, an almost-heartbeat that found Daniel's and slipped under it like a second current. When he pressed the cracked stone halves together in his pocket, heat pooled along the seam and throbbed in time.

"False morning," Ava said, slipping into the chair across from him like a shadow deciding to be a person. She had not slept. The whites of her eyes were threaded with red, and graphite dust stained the pads of her fingers. Her sketchbook lay half-open in her lap, a dark hinge.

"What does the second seal breaking mean?" Daniel asked. The question felt too large for the space between them.

"That the walls are thinner," she said without ceremony. "And the ones that know your name don't have to knock as hard."

He waited. She looked past him toward the corridor that led to the dayroom, toward the corner where the wall had breathed once when the power died. "The next stage will look like a choice," she added quietly. "You'll think not choosing is safe. It isn't."

He glanced at the sketchbook. She thumbed it open so he could see the newest page. The hospital hallways ran like arteries into trees; the trees crowded into the ward; shadows in both landscapes shared the same edges. Between them, a circle glowed, neither all forest nor all tile—stitched, like a wound that refused to decide how to heal.

A softness of footsteps, and Father Grayson took the seat beside them, his shoulders telling the story of a night spent in a chair and prayers said because they were the only rhythm left to keep time. "You two look like people who could use coffee," he said, and then, because there was none, "I can offer something stronger."

They moved to the quietest corner of the dayroom, where the window made a pale rectangle of sky pretend to be a view. Grayson folded his hands, not to perform, simply to keep them from carrying what they could not lift.

"When I was a young priest," he said, "I watched a man who swore he saw things the rest of us did not. He was not lying. He was not well. Both statements were true. We prayed. We fasted. We stayed. He died anyway, but not alone. Sometimes grace is not the ending; it's the during. Faith is a choice, Daniel. Not a trick for being unafraid."

Daniel found that the words did not make the room smaller. "Will you pray with them? With all of us?"

"Every night," Grayson said. "As long as they'll let me." He glanced toward Harker's office. "As long as anyone lets me."

It turned out Harker would. She called Daniel in before lunch, notepad on the desk but unopened, her expression the kind that comes after sleeping with the light on and deciding not to be embarrassed about it.

"I've been in the archives," she said without preamble. "Not online. Boxes. Paper. Dust that doesn't belong to my lifetime." She slid a photocopy across the desk. It was a typewritten memo from 1978, the letters crisp and cold: INCIDENT REPORT—SUBLEVEL CONSTRUCTION.

Contractor notes on "unexplained magnetism," tools jumping, cameras that wouldn't record, a crewman who claimed "the basement sings." A second page—handwritten, a social worker's scrawl—had one phrase underlined twice: The Breaker.

"It shows up in reports for decades," Harker said. "A name no one explains. Always near disappearances. Psychological collapses. It reads like a superstition until it shows up next to body counts."

Daniel touched the paper with the back of his finger, the way you touch a hot pan you don't trust. "You think The Breaker is... what we've seen."

"I think The Breaker is what the people who were here before us called what they could not control." Her voice thinned. "I think the seals you draw are not coming from your mind alone. And I think if we go further, we may not be able to put the lid back on."

"We don't have a lid," Daniel said, more sharply than he intended. "We have vanishing beds."

Harker stared at him for a long beat, something fierce flickering behind the fatigue. "Then we plan," she said. "We don't wander." She closed the file and didn't put it away. "And we do not go anywhere alone."

The hospital agreed with her in its own way. Lights popped without sound in the hallway at four o'clock, tiny bursts of glass like sotto voce applause. Doors to empty rooms sighed open and stood there, the air from within colder, as if each room had learned the trick of keeping weather. Security monitors in the nurses' station hiccuped into static whenever a shadow moved and returned to clarity with an innocence that felt like mockery.

Patients began reporting dreams they insisted weren't dreams. A woman whose hands shook too much to hold a fork described a faceless visitor who stood over her bed and spoke in syllables that made the inside of her head ache. A young man who never looked up from his slippers said a voice had leaned against his ear and told him to stop saying his name. None of them had spoken to each other; all of them said the visit happened at 3:07.

In the middle of the dayroom, Ava gave a small sound like a thread snapping. She folded inward, sketchbook clutched to her chest, and slid to the tile. Daniel and Grayson were there before anyone else; Harker arrived with a nurse who had the quick, steady hands of someone who could pick up a dropped heart and tuck it back in.

Ava's eyes were wide open, pupils blown. Her fingers moved without grace or aim, flinging pages. The floor filled with images—chapel seam, bell, the altar split like a wound; seals in tight succession, some Daniel knew, some that slid past recognition and made his blood feel too thin.

Then the page that held him: a clearing rendered in blunt, clean lines, and in its center a man with his arms out, head tipped back as if listening for rain. Symbols covered his skin like a second, more honest anatomy. He did not need a face to be identified. Ava's graphite had made him.

"The third one…" she gasped, voice like a paper cut. "It's coming for you."

He didn't argue. He didn't know how.

They got her onto a couch. Harker took her pulse, the nurse counted her breaths, Grayson whispered calm over the din of the hum, and Ava's eyes slid shut like doors closing in a house you've lived in so long you can walk it in the dark.

Evening slunk in, exhausted, and found no one ready for what it brought. Grayson started his prayers at nine, soft-voiced, standing where the ward could hear him if they wanted and ignore him if they couldn't. A handful of patients sat nearby; spines unbent for the first time in days. Harker didn't angle her office door closed.

Daniel sat on the edge of his bed and tried to decide whether he was more afraid of sleeping or not sleeping. The hum was formal now, one sustained tone that filled the room the way a single line can fill a page. He pressed the two halves of the stone together and felt their seam find its best possible fit, imperfect and stubborn, heat accumulating like a promise he hadn't made yet.

He did not mean to slip. There was no softening, no lid lowering over his eyes, no syrup between thought and breath. One moment he was in his room; the next he was in a hospital that had turned itself inside out.

Walls traded places with corridors. Doors hung where ceilings should be. The red emergency lights ran along the floor like veins. Every room he passed was occupied by shadow— shapes that moved as if they were remembering how to be bodies. Voices rode the hum now, not on top of it, but inside it, so that listening to the sound felt like drinking from a river that spoke your name between stones.

"Daniel," one voice said, the syllables tender and wrong. "Daniel," another said, and the tone was his own, thrown back from somewhere it shouldn't have learned to echo. He didn't answer. Ava's warning lived on his tongue like a splinter.

He turned a corner that should not have existed and found the door that should not have been here—the door to the chapel, lifted whole from the sublevel and set into this impossible hall. The carvings were deeper, the lines dark as if ink had been worked into the grain. The seam down its center pulsed with light no brighter than breath seen on a winter morning.

He reached out. His hand hovered an inch from the seam. Heat climbed from the stone halves in his pocket to the tendon inside his wrist, up his forearm, into the ache at his shoulder where fear slept when it was tired.

The hum paused, not stopped—paused—the way a musician lifts the bow to make room for the moment your breath decides whether to go in or out.

Daniel set his palm to the seam.

The door exhaled.

Chapter 19: The Third Seal

The door exhaled, and time slipped.

The seam under Daniel's palm warmed until the heat climbed his wrist and startled the muscle in his shoulder that fear liked to sleep in. The corridor around him doubled, blurred, then split—white walls running like water, red baseboard glow lengthening into the dark ribs of trees. The chapel door was both door and stone, its carved circles flaring like embers in a wind that wasn't there.

He stood in two places at once: the ward hall and the forest clearing, each laid over the other like a tracing. The earth inside the stone circle looked freshly cut, wounds scored into the dirt in the same spirals he'd drawn until his hands cramped; in the hospital, the scuffed tile reflected a faint, impossible shine, as if the floor remembered moon.

Whispers turned to weight. They orbited him, voices in distorted echoes, as if someone had recorded his name and his daughter's and played them back through water and wire.

Da—niel.

Daddy.

Daniel.

Each syllable carried a small hook. He clenched his hand over the seam and didn't answer, because Ava's warning lived on his tongue like a splinter he refused to pull.

Lily stood just beyond the circle's glow. She was seven forever in this light, Bun-Bun tucked under her arm, hair tangled the way morning left it before Emily's fingers found the part. Her chest rose and fell too fast, the way it did after a run down the hall to make him laugh.

"You can't run from this, Daddy," she said, and her voice— clearer here than dreams allowed—put a fault line through him. "They've already marked you."

She pointed at his hands.

He looked. Under his skin, faint and ember-warm, symbols traced themselves like veins he hadn't known were there. Rings and ribs, a geometry of belonging he hadn't agreed to and couldn't scrub away.

The hospital snapped back sharp for an instant, the clearing's light fading like a memory you hold too tightly. A light overhead popped with a dry crack; glass snowed the hall. A monitor screamed, and then its shriek broke off like a throat had closed. Plaster flaked the seam of the ceiling and fell soft as ash. Somewhere a door slammed its opinion against its frame and then tried again. Ava's feet were already pounding toward him. Father Grayson's voice rose, sure and steady, the way a line holds a ship.

"Daniel!"

Hands seized his elbow—Ava's nails, cold and urgent; Grayson's grip warm and anchoring. They pulled, and the door under his palm tugged back like undertow.

The hum that had lived in the walls drew itself upright and roared. The ward shook in a way that had nothing to do with weather, a depth-rattle that suggested the building had bones and something was knocking on them from inside. Plaster cracked along a clean seam and sifted down in lazy veils. The baseboard glow hiccuped and went thin and red.

He tried to let go.

The door opened for him.

It didn't swing—it unlocked forward, seam breathing wider until the slabs parted on their own. The black beyond wasn't emptiness; it was a presence clothed as distance. Cold rolled out in a low fog that hugged the tile and licked around his shoes like a tide with teeth.

From the dark, something shaped like a voice spoke his name in a ruin of tenderness.

"Daniel. Come and see."

The words went through him, not to him, and with them came warmth that didn't belong to the hall—the remembered temperature of Emily's palm covering his on a steering wheel while Lily slept open-mouthed in the back seat; the faint flour-dust texture of kitchen air at Christmas; the small thud of a child's head finding his shoulder and deciding it was a pillow. The dark wore these like a good coat.

He staggered toward it, just half a step, the way a thirsty man leans toward a sink. The muscles in his forearm tightened; his palm pushed harder into the seam because want is a weight, and his body mistook it for balance.

"Daniel." Ava's voice tried for command and hit plea. Her grip slid to his wrist, nails biting until fresh crescents rose. "Don't."

"Stay," Grayson said, the word aimed past Daniel's ears into whatever else was listening.

A breath of cold stroked Daniel's face, intimate as a whisper under a blanket. The black did not threaten. It confided. A scent rose—cinnamon, rain in Emily's braid, the warm plastic of an old night-light. The syllables of a name formed of their own accord in his mouth, shaped by love, not by bravado. "Em—"

Ava's hand snapped up and clapped over his lips, harder than a friend should. Pain flared. The almost-name dissolved on his tongue like sugar in scalding water. Her eyes were huge and wet and furious. "Not them," she said into his breath. "Never them."

Shame hit fast and clean. It made room for fear to sit down beside it and breathe without owning the room.

Vision found him again, harder this time, like a hand over his eyes pressing until stars flared. The clearing jumped forward years and fell backward in the same blink. He saw a tent with the rain-fly off because Lily had wanted the constellations and Emily had smiled and said yes to one more ridiculous thing. He saw the trees—God help him, he saw the trees—with faint loops and crosses scorched on their trunks where no fire had touched, marks subtle enough to dismiss in daylight and obvious as a shout under the wrong moon.

148

The smooth, faceless shape stepped between trees. Not a walking, exactly. A deciding to be closer. It didn't need features to project its attention. Only its tilt—the same curious angle he'd seen outside his ward door, the way of listening that made it feel as if it were reading his fear off the air.

"Lily!" Emily's voice broke the night the way light breaks glass.

He fell through the moment as if the ground had been yanked back an inch. The hall returned, his knees against tile, the seam slick under his palm. Ava knelt in front of him with her face too pale and too steady, one hand on his shoulder, the other pressed to his sternum like she could keep his heart from bolting. Father Grayson stood with a hand splayed over Daniel's head as men bless and steady at once, his other hand open in the air as if holding off a crowd he preferred not to see.

"Back," Grayson said to the black, not to Daniel. He spoke like a man who expected obedience from weather.

Behind them, the dark at the door's mouth thickened without moving. Frost crawled a delicate lace along the threshold and then retreated, as if deciding this surface wasn't the one it wanted yet. Somewhere down the corridor, someone sobbed the word no until it ceased to be language and became a pattern.

Alarms found their lungs again and barked in staggered pairs. The red exit signs stuttered. The hum didn't swell; it deepened until Daniel felt it cross a boundary inside him and begin to vibrate the symbols under his skin like strings.

"Close it!" Harker's voice cut hard and close. She was suddenly there, breath clouding, flashlight in one hand—its beam a weak finger swallowed at the edges by the dark—her other hand already reaching for a latch that had not been present until she'd decided there must be one. She found a metal tongue at the frame's throat and slammed it home. The door did not shut. It shook, amused.

"Back," she said to all of them, without looking away. "Back now."

Ava hauled Daniel by the elbow; Grayson bounded to the side of the frame and pressed his shoulder into wood. He began to pray so low Daniel felt the words more than heard them, a thrum braided under the building's. Harker's jaw tightened. "On three," she said, as if force were a language the door might respect. "One. Two—"

The door slammed with them and without them, as if bored. The seam sealed. The hall breathed out a little.

Silence didn't return. Order didn't return. The ward erupted into its own liturgy. Names, shouted and answered and not answered. The sound of running that tried not to be running. A nurse's voice: "Room twelve—empty." Another: "Room nine—burn marks on the mattress." A third, shaking: "He was there. He was there."

Daniel rested his head against the cool wall and let the shame ebb without letting it turn into consent. His hands blazed softly beneath the skin, the inkless fire rising to the surface in pulses that aligned with the hum. In his pocket the broken prayer stone halves warmed until he thought they might fuse of their own accord.

Harker crouched, eye to eye, the flashlight idle now in her lap. She was shaken and refused to be disassembled by it. "What did you open?" she asked, not as accusation, but as triage.

"It opened to me," he said, and heard the childishness and didn't have a grown man's words to replace it. "It said—" He swallowed. "Come and see."

"Of course it did," Harker said, mouth flattening. Then command returned to her spine. "Count. Document scorch marks. Seal this hall." To Daniel: "You do not touch that seam again."

He nodded because anything else in his throat would have been confession or plea.

The inventory got worse and then stopped getting worse only because there weren't enough people left to lose. Two beds empty that had been full; a clean oval burned into a pillow like a kiss from a hot iron; a symbol charred above a headboard—two circles braided with a small bar where they crossed—still faintly warm when Harker pressed the back of her hand near it and snatched away with a hiss.

Security footage? Static.

Ava gathered fallen drawings into a messy stack. One found its way face-up between them: the corridor that didn't exist in any blueprint, drawn with the certainty of someone who had seen it and wished she hadn't. The circle at its end sat like a bell without sound.

"You've seen it now," she said. "The path below. They won't stop until you finish this."

"Finish it how?" he asked, not because he thought she knew—because his mouth needed a question to hold.

"With the seam that breaks and the seam that mends," she said, childlike and furious. "With choosing."

Grayson stood. The lines of his face had become the kind that come only when a man has pressed against nights like this and not backed up. "Then we finish it on our terms," he said. "With faith, not fear."

"And with a plan," Harker added. "Maps. Locks. Fewer accidents."

Daniel looked down at his trembling hands, at the dim, steady fire beneath his skin finding the same measure as the hum in the walls. The sound had settled back, quieter, yes, but no longer distant. It nested now. It had learned his room, his ribs, his name.

He closed his fingers around the broken stone halves until the edges bit and heat pulsed at their seam.

"Come and see," the dark had said.

"All right," he whispered—not to it, but to the God he could not hear above the noise unless he whispered first. "But on Your light."

The hum held steady, as if listening.

Somewhere down the hall, a clock moved past 3:07 without stopping and made almost a full minute feel like a gift.

Chapter 20: Shattered Alliances

Morning arrived like a decision no one in the building had voted on. The hallways went through the motions—linens traded, meds logged, coffee poured into flimsy cups—but the quiet had a bruise under it. The hum that used to belong to the ward now traveled with Daniel. He felt it when he leaned on a doorjamb, when he pressed his palm to his pocket, even when he closed his eyes: not sound exactly, but a pressure, personal and precise, as if the walls had learned his pulse and were keeping time with it.

Staff spoke in the soft, trimmed sentences of people who didn't want to startle the air. Patients drifted, eyes catching on corners. Where the door to the chapel had been last night, only plaster stared back—fresh, smooth, indecently whole.

"Daniel." Harker stood at her office door. Not a summons. A request wrapped in steel.

Inside, dust swam in a strip of gray from half-open blinds. She didn't reach for a pen. Her hands pressed flat on a thin folder, bracing it like a table in an earthquake.

"I went deeper into the archives," she said. "Past what's digitized. Past what anyone intends for a hospital director to find when she can't sleep." She slid a brittle sheet toward him. An index card, browned at the edges, its typewritten lines marching with mid-century certainty:

WING D—FILES REMOVED.

CONTAINMENT—NOT CARE.

TRANSFER ALL INCIDENTS TO "STRUCTURAL/UTILITY."

"There are references to an entire wing of records that don't exist anymore," she said. "Not lost. Erased. What's left says this place was built as a box before it was a hospital. Containment came first. Healing was a cover."

Daniel touched the card with the back of his finger, as if direct contact might burn. "So you don't think this is just us seeing patterns in grief."

Harker's composure cracked like glass under heat. "I no longer believe this is only trauma," she admitted, each word slow as confession. "I still believe in brains. I also believe something inside this building keeps pressing the lid."

He exhaled, and the sound was too much like relief. "Then we're on the same page."

"No." Her mouth twitched as if to say more and then didn't. "We're on the same page for five minutes. Then we're back to choices that all look like mistakes."

The fragile truce broke as the others entered. Father Grayson came first, Bible under his arm, jaw tight. Ava slipped behind him, sketchbook hugged to her ribs, graphite smeared into her skin like oil.

"We go back down," Ava said flatly, no prelude. "They won't stop. The path is open. We need to know what the fifth looks like before it looks at us."

"With covering," Grayson countered, hand firm on the Bible as if it had heartbeat. "With prayer. With fasting. With more light than bravado."

"Prayer didn't close the door last night," Ava snapped, eyes sharp as glass.

"It kept us from falling through it," he returned, steady but stung.

Daniel's hands betrayed him—faintly glowing, as though embers had found a home beneath his skin. He tucked them under his forearms. "We plan," he said, hearing Harker's

157

cadence in his own mouth. "We don't wander. We don't go alone."

Ava's stare shifted to him, hard, accusing. "You don't get to sound like her, Daniel. This started following you. Don't pretend you're just one of us—it wants you."

The words hit like a slap. Harker's jaw tightened; she didn't deny it. Grayson shifted uncomfortably but didn't defend him either. For one raw second Daniel stood alone, accused, his allies weighing silence instead of loyalty.

The ward chose that moment to answer them. Lights flickered indecisively, then blew out in a line down the dayroom. Two doors slammed, then swung wide again like mouths testing vowels. Shadows stayed after their owners moved, refusing to dissipate.

By lunchtime, chaos bloomed. Patients muttered in braided unison; syllables bent into a language older than their throats. One man clutched his bedrail and shrieked, "Don't say your name where it can hear you!" An elderly woman clawed at her forearms until Harker caught her wrists, whispering calm into the storm.

Then Ava went rigid, eyes too wide, voice not her own: "The path is open. The fifth comes. Choose your light before the dark chooses for you."

Grayson surged up, chair clattering back. "You do not have permission!" he thundered, but the air answered only with more whispers.

Daniel staggered toward the window. The hum wasn't outside anymore. It was inside, nested in his thought scaffolds. Promises slid through his ribs like knives wrapped in velvet: I can give her back. Both of them. Don't you want to know? Didn't you always want to know?

He saw the circle in the woods without closing his eyes. Emily and Lily stood inside it this time—solemn, watching him. His lips moved before he knew he had given them permission. The first syllable of the forbidden name formed, fragile and treacherous, trembling on his tongue.

"Daniel." Harker's hand clamped his shoulder. Not gentle. Not ungentle. Just enough to break the spell. "Come back."

He flinched, realizing he had nearly spoken the word. The horror of how close he had come hollowed his chest. Ava sagged against the couch, gasping. Grayson pressed his palm to the wall, head bowed, as if listening for a carpenter's crack before the wood gives.

Evening limped in. The ward gathered itself into uneasy silence, the kind that feels borrowed. Harker authorized

Grayson's prayer hour but stayed in the circle herself, her folded hands betraying what her voice would not admit. Ava sat in her chair, wrists bandaged, staring at Daniel with a mix of pity and warning.

Daniel turned the fractured stone in his palm. Its seam glowed faintly, a reminder and a rebuke. He had almost said it. Almost.

The silence that pressed in was not peace. It was pressure. Attention. Waiting for him to slip again.

Chapter 21: The Hollow Silence

Silence had a shape. It pressed from the corners, filling the seams the hum used to occupy, a patient weight that made every small noise sound like a sin. The ward wore it like a shroud. No mechanical thrum, no low vibration in the vents, just the thin tinnitus of fluorescent bulbs and the honest sounds of breath and rubber soles and the faint drag of a sleeve across a doorframe.

Daniel moved carefully, like a man who had woken with an animal sleeping on his chest and didn't dare startle it. In his pocket, the prayer stone lay whole and warm, a pulse that was not his. The ash letters over the sink—FOUR—looked fresher in the morning light, the strokes clean and matte, as if written with a fingertip that knew its own pressure.

Harker came in without knocking.

She shut the door with her foot and stood a beat to find her voice. She had a tablet under one arm, her blazer rumpled, hair bent wrong from being gripped in the dark. Professional armor hung on her, dented and lighter than it should be.

"I have footage," she said. Fury put scaffolding under the words, but fear had done the building. "You should see it."

She set the tablet on the dresser and queued up the feed. A black-and-white pane of his room unfurled. Daniel watched himself sleep—on his side, knees drawn, the blanket half-kicked to the floor. The clock in the corner marked a slow minute. Nothing moved.

Then the ash lifted.

Not from a tray, not from a hand. From nowhere—gathering in the air like gnats and then aligning, a cloud teaching itself to write. The word assembled letter by letter, each stroke appearing in the space where it would have gone if a finger had made it. F took shape, then O, then U, then R. The ash settled with the neat, satisfied grace of a finished signature. Daniel did not stir.

Harker froze the frame. She didn't look at the screen. She looked at him, and for the first time since he had met her, he saw the naked thing under competence: outrage on behalf of her house, her people, her own mind.

"I cannot treat this," she said, softly. "I can count it. I can record it. I can keep you from falling down the stairwell. But I cannot medicate a word onto a wall when no hand is in the room."

Daniel sat on the bed like a student called to the front of the class for a lesson no one had written. "Then we stop pretending it's only inside my head," he said. The admission carried its own kind of despair.

Harker barked a laugh that wasn't laughter. "We stopped last night. I just… needed to say it out loud. To hear what it sounded like in the air."

He nodded. "Like a truth," he said. "Like a verdict."

She lifted the tablet. "Like we're past containment."

They both flinched when the intercom clicked for a second and died. The silence rushed back in, polite and sharp.

He found Ava in the dayroom, tucked into her corner with the sketchbook already open, graphite grinding dark crescents under her fingernails. Her hair had braided itself into chaos. She didn't look up when he sat.

"Listen," she whispered. "Hear it?"

He listened and heard nothing. The nothing had teeth.

"The quiet is their favorite part," she said, voice too low for anyone else. "It's the sound of teeth before they bite."

She turned the page. The drawing hit him like cold. A circle, but not the others; this one jagged along one edge, as if something had taken a piece out of it and left it hungry. Around the circle, spirals, not clean rings but warped, stretched—figures threaded through them like they'd been woven from a single long line. The graphite dark fluttered where her hand had dug in.

"The fourth," she said. Her hand trembled. "It isn't waiting for you anymore. It's coming through."

He thought of the word on his wall. He thought of the silence holding its breath. "Then we're inside its timing," he said.

"We always were," she answered, and it wasn't cruelty. It was weather.

Grayson arrived with the kind of fatigue that makes men compassionate instead of mean. He had circles under his eyes and a spine that wouldn't bow, and when he saw the drawing he crossed himself without embarrassment.

"Boundaries," he said, almost to himself. He turned to Daniel. "We set them. We hold them. We pray like we mean it."

Ava's head tipped, weary and sharp. "We go down," she said. "Prayer at the door won't keep a house that built itself around the door."

Grayson met her, not flinching. "Prayer is not at the door," he said evenly. "Prayer is the light you carry when the door opens. You know that."

"Then carry it," she said. "Just... carry it while we move."

Their eyes touched for a long, taut second. Daniel felt the heat of the argument but not its ugliness. It wasn't a fight about belief. It was a fight about sequence and risk and which kind of courage would be required first.

Harker tried to be a director, then set the role down because the stage had changed. "If we go below," she said, steadying her voice into something operational, "we do it in pairs, with radios that may or may not work, and we mark our path like we're walking into a mine. We plan a return before we take a step forward. We don't chase sounds."

"Agreed," Grayson said. Ava nodded once, reluctant but real.

The silence watched them compromise.

By noon, the building's manners failed. A slam shuddered down the restricted wing, then another and another, doors throwing themselves open and shut like an argument in a house you don't want to be a child in. Overhead lights flickered with the speed of a sick heartbeat. Three bulbs exploded in shy pops, sprinkling glass like sleet. A nurse swore softly in Spanish and kept moving.

Then came the voices. Not patients. Not staff. The intercom crackled and coughed static into the room, a low snow through which other sounds threaded—leaves being walked through, the far-off grind of insects, and, for one lancing second, a small girl's laugh. Lily's. Daniel's name followed, drawn out and doubled, like someone calling in a canyon and getting the echo wrong.

He turned away. He kept his mouth shut.

Rooms filled and emptied of frenzy. Patients who never spoke sat up in bed and chanted in slow, childlike unison: "The fourth comes. The fourth comes." Harker went room to room, saying names, giving hands to hold onto, re-teaching breath. Grayson set himself in the middle of the ward with all

166

the humility of a man who knows his tool looks ridiculous in a flood and picked it up anyway. "Lord, be near," he said, and then again. "Lord, keep." His voice made space.

Daniel slipped. It was not a decision. It was how a step carries forward when the floor has been tugged half an inch back. The hall broke, remade itself wrong. Walls leaned closer, paint breathing shallow. Doors stretched into tall, narrow ovals, cathedral windows corrupting their own shapes. The red baseboard glow bled up the wall like a wound finally remembering to seep.

He blinked and was in the clearing. The stone circle was cracked, light bleeding from the seams in thin rivers. Trees bent away. The faceless figure stood just outside the broken ring, head tipped, listening. Lily was there and not there—older, somehow, a few inches taller, her face lengthened into the teenager he would never meet. Her eyes were not void this time; they were cold with a certainty that hurt him worse.

"The last choice is already made," she said, and the words fogged the air like a winter breath.

"What choice?" he asked, and his voice made him ashamed with how quickly it clothed itself in panic. "Who made it?"

Her mouth moved around the ghost of a smile that had nothing to do with joy. "You did," she said, and then everything pulled like a tide changing its mind.

He came back hard. Ava's fingers were clamped around his shoulders, nails biting through fabric. "Daniel!" Her face was inches away, blown pupils and tears she didn't know about. "Stay with me."

He swallowed something iron. "I'm here," he lied, then corrected himself: "I'm… almost here."

The day leaned toward evening like a door leaning toward a hinge. The quiet tightened. Staff moved faster without running. Harker ordered the restricted wing sealed and then stood in front of the sealed doors like a person willing to be a sign. Grayson asked for the lights in the dayroom to be left higher than usual and no one argued.

Night eased in with the softness of a hand that means to press hard. The repaired stone warmed in Daniel's pocket until the heat downshifted into glow. He sat on his bed, back against the wall, listening to the silence listen back.

The first boom came like a slow punch to the soles of his feet. Not thunder. It rose from below, a single deep shift as if an old machine had engaged a gear it had waited a century to find. The second followed and sat under the first. The third made the bed frame answer with a low, sympathetic hum.

Down the hall, someone cried out—no word, just the sound a body makes when a line tightens—and then quiet again, the heavy kind that has already chosen and doesn't need to ask permission.

Daniel closed his hand around the whole stone until the heat bit and held.

"The fourth is coming," he whispered, because saying it aloud felt like setting a table for an unwanted guest and he had been taught to be polite even to things that meant him harm.

Somewhere far below, something answered with a rumble so old it felt like a memory learning to speak. Every light in the ward hiccuped. Then, like a set of lungs exhaling, they went out together and stayed out, and the dark came down not like a curtain but like a lid.

Chapter 22: Into the Dark

The dark came down like a lid.

No emergency glow along the baseboards. No dim pulse from the nurse's station. No hum. Just the soft click of metal cooling in the ducts and the breathing of a dozen people who didn't want to hear themselves be alive.

Daniel opened his hand. The prayer stone answered him like a held breath finally let go—no blaze, just a low, steady glow that turned his palm into a small, warm lantern. It threw a circle of honeyed light on his knees, on the edge of the bed, on the ash word over the sink. FOUR watched him from the wall, gray and clean, as if it had been written for this darkness alone.

"Count off!" Harker's voice cut through the black, sharp and steady. "Nurses—flashlights up, keep them low. Move patients to the dayroom; keep hands on shoulders. No one runs; no one screams."

She moved like a lighthouse, her cheap penlight stuttering a weak cone. The beam caught faces—startled, wet-eyed, furious—and slid on. Staff answered in clipped calls. Names rose and were returned. A sob collapsed into breath.

Somewhere a plastic cup fell, rolled, stopped. The silence took the room back between sounds, heavy as a shut door.

"Lord, be near," Father Grayson said, not loud, not performative. He stood in the center of the ward with both hands open, as if receiving instead of fending. The words sank and steadied, adding weight where panic had been skimming the surface.

Ava found Daniel by the shape his light made. She came close enough that he could see the graphite on her fingertips, the new rawness at her wrists where symbols had bloomed like burns. Her eyes looked bigger in the glow.

"It's not a blackout," she breathed. "It's a hand. They've put their hand over the house."

He felt the truth of it like a draft you can't line up to find. The stone vibrated once, a quiet click in his bones, and tugged his palm toward the corridor that led to STAFF ONLY and the stairwell below.

"You feel it," Ava said, watching his wrist tilt as if pulled by a string.

"Yes."

Grayson came to them without their calling him. His face looked carved from the same kind of decision Harker's voice had. "If you go," he said, "you don't go alone."

"You can't all go down there," Harker countered, appearing from the dark with the conviction of a person who has made a choice while the rest of the room argued. "We need bodies up here. We need order."

"We need both," Grayson said. "You need me up here. You know it."

Harker knew it. She flinched anyway, the way a person flinches when a good idea will cost. "Fine. I go." She angled her light to keep all their faces in it. "We go. Short. We mark and return. We don't chase sounds." She met Daniel's eyes. "You do not touch anything that breathes."

He nodded, guilty in advance.

They moved. The stone's glow got them to the STAFF ONLY door; Harker's keycard found the reader by muscle memory. The lock clicked in the stillness like a tongue against teeth. They slipped through and shut the hospital's ordinary behind them.

The stairwell air had a cellar's temperature and an old church's smell: wet stone braided into something sweeter that might have been incense or might have been rot pretending. The dark wasn't as complete down here; the stone's glow reached farther, a soft bell on each step. Their footfalls sounded wrong—muffled and close, with no echo—as if the walls had their hands up, catching the noise.

"Listen," Ava whispered.

Daniel did. The silence had a grain to it now, a slow tide moving under the stillness. If the hum was gone, something had replaced it—a pressure in the marrow, a rhythm you felt in the teeth before you heard it. It wasn't sound; it was intent.

The sublevel corridor received them with breath held. The maintenance cage hunched to the left, wire dark with old damp. To the right, the corridor bent into the part of the hospital the blueprints disliked to remember. Harker kept her light low and angled, skimming the floor. "Mark," she said.

Ava bent, dragged a stick of charcoal along the wall. A simple line, a hash, another—primitive breadcrumbs. It looked like vandalism and felt like prayer.

The farther they went, the more the space laid its wrongness out like a map. Corners didn't meet cleanly. The ceiling bowed the way a tired back does. The air got colder without moving. The stone in Daniel's hand grew warmer, its glow deepening until it wasn't light so much as presence, colorless and constant, the kind a person can stand inside and call by name without using one.

They reached the door with the wired-glass window. The reliquary closet beyond showed them its monkish inventory in the stone's glow: the bell black with tarnish, the cracked white candles, the small cross with its seared arm. Ava's gaze snagged there and tried to stay.

"Don't," Harker said gently, as if pulling a child away from a rail.

At the end of the corridor, the chapel door waited, the carved circles deeper than Daniel remembered, as if fingers had worked the grooves all night while the ward thought it was sleeping. The seam down the center breathed cold.

"Boundaries," Grayson said quietly. "We set them here. We do not ask the room what it wants to show us. We tell it what it is allowed."

He stepped to the threshold and began in a voice that had become the building's other weather: promises and petitions, the old words that lay a line on the floor and dare the dark to step over it. Harker stood to his left, shoulders squared to the door, light low. Ava put her palm on the wall the way you lay a hand on a horse to let it smell you.

Daniel lifted the stone to the seam the way a person lifts a candle to another flame. He did not touch. He let the light meet the line.

The room opened anyway.

It didn't swing. It relented. The seam slipped, the halves of the door sighing past each other like shoulders giving way in a narrow hall. Cold spilled out and around their ankles, animal-low. The chapel had been empty last time. Now it breathed.

Symbols on the walls brightened by a shade, as if remembering their original ink. Not pulses, not theatrics. A faint, living saturation. The pews sagged farther under a weight that wasn't weight. The altar had split wide—where there had been a seam, now there was a wound, a bright line of something like light and like heat and like none of the words Daniel knew, spilling a steady, molten glow into the seam's shadow.

They crossed the threshold.

The glow from the altar made the stone's light unnecessary, but Daniel couldn't bring himself to close his hand. The heat from the wound in the altar wasn't heat the air could describe; it was a pressure the body translated as fever and fever-dream at once. His skin prickled. The marks under it stirred like fish in shallow water.

The chapel noticed them. Not an idea—an attention. Paper lifted on a breath that wasn't wind; old bulletins and log sheets skated across the floor like leaves on a pond's skin. The unlit candles leaned a fraction, as if to hear better. From somewhere in the stone, a whisper that might have been the building's bones settling became a whisper that might have been voices pretending to be that.

"Hold," Harker said, as if she could convince time to wait its turn.

Ava doubled over with a small sound, hands to her wrists. The marks there—thin ribs of circles, the bracelets the hospital kept adding to her—flared and reddened as if pressed from underneath. She hissed through her teeth and looked up at Daniel, eyes glass-bright.

"They're singing through me," she said, and he could see how not-metaphor the words were.

Grayson stepped closer, palm out. "You do not have permission," he said to the room, to the thing behind it, to all the nameless and named somewhere in between. "This house is not yours."

The altar shuddered. The split widened a finger's width. Light bled with more insistence. The chapel air thickened like water about to boil.

The hum returned.

Not the house's low, familiar drone. This was larger, layered—depths stacked in the same sound, an ocean under an earthquake under a note drawn by a bow on a string the size of a bridge. It carried voices tucked inside it the way a current carries reeds—fragments of prayer, pleas, laughter, Lily's bright clear Daddy laid next to Daniel's name until the two were thread and needle and wound.

The pew nearest the aisle cracked with a clean pop and slumped into itself. A shower of rotten wood dust drifted like pollen. The reliquary bell inside its closet rang once without moving, a single pure tone that made Daniel's teeth ache.

He staggered. The chapel doubled, then tripled—the forest laid over it, the circle superimposed on the altar's wound, the hospital's long white corridors stitched in like a lattice across both. The light from the altar and the light from the circle and the light from the prayer stone met and argued, and for a second he saw how small a difference words made when light was deciding things.

Lily stood in the circle, older again—taller by inches that felt like miles, hair longer, face thinned into the lines of a teenager. She didn't look like a ghost; she looked like a photograph taken from the wrong end of a life. Her expression wouldn't give him what he begged for—no smile, no rage, no forgiveness, nothing as legible as grief. It was the look people get when they've realized there's only one road and you're not walking it with them.

"It's almost over," she said. "But you don't know which of us will survive it."

He faltered, wanting to bargain with whatever part of the air would take currency. The hum climbed by a hair. The stone in his hand seared. He didn't let go.

The room convulsed.

Papers lifted in a heave; logbooks jumped and slammed; the bench backs split along old hairline cracks as if a hand had run the length of them, testing each seam for failure. Scratchings ran along the walls where there was nothing to scratch. Candle wicks smoked without flame. The bell rang again, twice, as if it had been struck and then corrected itself to a different key.

Ava screamed. It wasn't long; it wasn't theatrical. The sound was the exact length of pain. She cradled her wrists. The marks there had gone from red to white-hot, skin welted in perfect circles like a brand shaped by grammar.

Grayson's prayer stuttered and resumed. "Mercy," he said, voice rough now. "Mercy. Mercy." It did not sound like asking; it sounded like a man standing between a door and the people behind him and telling the door what it will and will not do.

Harker raised her light like a baton. "We retreat," she ordered, as if command could bend physics. "Now. Daniel—move."

He didn't. Something in him, older than fear and uglier than courage, rooted his feet. The sound inside the sound—the deep one, the one that had called him at the door—rose like a name translating itself into a human throat.

The crack in the altar widened. A line of white poured out, too bright to be seen and too dim to be called light. The hum pressed so hard that the edges of things blurred—pews, walls, people—and the chapel became idea and pressure and weather.

The fourth seal broke.

They felt it. Not a noise alone—a shear, a rending along a line that had waited to be found. The floor trembled; dust flew in a fine, excited haze. The reliquary bell rang a third time and didn't stop ringing, though nothing touched it. A low, darker-than-dark shape coiled around the altar's base—not smoke, not shadow, something that swallowed light without being the absence of it. Grayson swore under his breath and took a step forward as if he could convince that physics to try decency.

"Run!" Harker's voice tore her throat on the way out. "Move!"

Ava stumbled for the aisle; eyes blind with tears she didn't register. Grayson grabbed her elbow and hauled. Harker shoved the door wider with her shoulder and didn't care if the wood wanted to splinter. The chapel's attention pivoted—Daniel felt it like a searchlight moving, then finding.

He stepped toward the altar.

He didn't decide to. He saw later that decision had been made farther back, in a place made of promises he'd said out loud and ones he'd never dared to. The line that had run through the house, through the ward, through the marks under his skin, through the bell and the book and the boy he had been, led there, like a seam that asks for a hand.

"Daniel!" Harker, furious, terrified. "No."

He put the stone over the wound.

It split. Not like before. Not like a break does when it fails. It opened like a seed—clean, inevitable, a hinge finding the angle it had been cut for. Light—not light—poured through the crack in a sheet so complete that for a second the room had no features, only an inside and an outside trading places at the speed of breath.

Sound stopped.

No hum, no prayers, no paper, no bell. Even the memory of sound held still, as if someone had set a glass over the moment and taken the air out.

White.

Not color. Not even light. A blank so present it laid its hand on every shape and told it to tell the truth or vanish. Daniel's hand burned and didn't; the stone in his grip weighed everything and nothing; the floor under his feet existed and then didn't, the way faith does when it is not propped up by outcomes.

For a single beat, he thought: Let it be Your light. Not theirs. Not mine.

The blank swallowed the thought and kept it.

Then everything imploded into that white, and there was no room, no altar, no door, no hum, no Harker, no Grayson, no Ava, no FOUR—only a silence so absolute it made God sound like a whisper behind the eyes.

Chapter 23: The White Room

White swallowed direction, then meaning, then time.

Daniel didn't fall. Falling presumes a down. He simply existed inside a blank so complete that even memory had to ask permission to knock. No hum. No air moving. The absence wasn't empty; it was attentive, like a closed eye that still sees light through the lid.

He looked for his hands and found them by heat. The prayer stone—whole a moment ago, broken a lifetime ago—sat in his palms and was both things at once. It throbbed without light, a heartbeat inside a heartbeat. When he pressed the halves together, there was no seam. When he let them part, a hairline opened and the white leaned in to consider.

A thought rose, naked and uncrafted. Let it be Your light. Not theirs. Not mine.

The white changed temperature. Not warmer. Known.

"Daniel."

The voice did not come from ahead or behind. It arrived everywhere at once, like a word spoken inside bone. It spoke his name the way a surgeon says scalpel or a locksmith says turn—not to summon, but to use.

He did not answer. He remembered Ava's warning like a splinter kept on purpose.

The white thinned. A shape slid forward—not a figure, not a face; a tilt, as if attention itself had leaned in to listen. The pressure around his head increased by a breath, a glove being pulled on.

You asked why, said the not-voice. The syllables wore his own cadence, then Lily's, then a dozen others he couldn't name. Every door opens to a question. You've spent your life knocking. Let me open. Let me answer.

He thought of chapter-one Daniel, in a folding chair the morning after a doctorate, hungry for certainties he could shelve. He thought of how easily why becomes worship, how quickly a man can mistake knowledge for safety.

He made himself breathe. "There are questions that are prayers," he said into the white. "And prayers that aren't questions at all."

Silence contracted. For a flash he felt hands he did not possess grip a ledge and hold. The presence came closer.

You opened the fourth, it said, with the bland mercy of a ledger. The next are not doors. They are thresholds. Step, and you will not need faith. You will have fact. Lily back in a kitchen with cinnamon in the air. Emily humming with rain in her hair. No more missing. No more fault lines.

Cinnamon bloomed in his head so vividly he had to swallow. For one treacherous moment he felt Emily's warmth against his shoulder, Lily's laughter bright in the next room. His mouth opened, her name nearly escaping like a sob.

He clenched his jaw until it ached. He let the want stand up in him and didn't pretend not to see it. He let it breathe. He did not kneel to it.

"If you could give," he said, surprised to hear his voice steady, "you wouldn't have to bargain."

The white trembled, infinitesimally, like a pond's skin when a dragonfly lands. He felt rather than heard the break in the rhythm—the first proof the thing could be refused.

You carry marks, it said, shifting tactics. We traced them into you because you were soft clay. Your need. Your hunger. Your why. The first seal was not a night. The first seal was a boy who learned to listen for doors.

A kitchen blurred through the white—plastic plates stacked two by two; a fridge with a cartoon magnet; silence that got loud at supper. He saw himself ten years old, counting the hours between a promise and an engine that never came up the drive. He felt again the inward lean toward any sound that might explain why being chosen sometimes looks exactly like being left.

"Maybe," he said. "But the mark isn't ownership. It's a map."

The presence tipped, puzzled, then amused. A map implies a destination. You are already here.

"Maps also show where not to go," he answered.

Nothing moved, because nothing existed that could. Still, he felt the white consult itself. In the pause he took inventory the way Grayson had taught him: fingers—warm; lungs—working; fear—present, but not driving; prayer—unfinished and therefore honest.

He raised the broken-perfect stone. "I don't know how to seal what's broken," he said to God and to the room and to the thing that wanted his mouth. "But I know how to hand You the seam."

The blank flexed—impatience, or calculation, or the simple physics of a will pressing on another. *Say my name*, it coaxed, casual as a friend teaching a password. *Names are doors. You know mine. You have drawn me. You have fed me syllables with your questions for years. Say it, and I will sit in your voice and sing your lost back into the room.*

A memory unfolded without consent: night over Old Rag. The circle, unbroken then. Lily's small fingers in his, the touch so ordinary he had not memorized it properly. The smooth-faced thing between trees, head tilted, the precise attention of a predator that has decided you are interesting.

Ava: Don't speak to them. Don't let them in.

Grayson: Prayer is the light you carry when the door opens.

Emily, once, in the kitchen dark: We can't know everything's why, Dan. We can know what love does.

He laughed—because love is ridiculous in a room like this and still the only non-absurd thing he knew. "I'm done naming you," he said, not with fury, not with bravado, but with the weariness of a man laying down a bad tool. "I will name what I belong to."

He lifted the stone high as if it were a candle in a church. "Jesus," he said, not as a charm, not as punctuation—as address. "Yours."

The white licked inward like flame meeting wind. A pressure left his head, sudden enough to sting. In the afterspace, other sounds arrived: the bell, wood groaning, a woman's ragged breath. The blank thinned, not dismissed; the seam he had offered tightened beneath his palms as if fingers stronger than his had joined him at the task.

A second voice entered the white, so quiet that if he had been shouting he would have missed it.

"Daddy."

It was not coaxing. Not bait. A fact.

Lily stood in the same not-space the presence had filled, as impossible and unornamented as grief. She was both seven and fifteen, the math refusing to behave. Bun-Bun hung by one ear. She looked at the stone, then at his face.

"You can't fix it," she said, solemn as a doctor with a clipboard. "You can forgive it."

He wanted to say forgive who. He wanted to say forgive me. He wanted to ask the aching, obvious are you— and stopped, because answers have their own appetites.

"I'm sorry," he said. The words fell into the white and did not echo because they had work to do. "For needing why more than I needed love. For trying to prize you out of the hand that holds you because I couldn't stand not being that hand. For letting the mark tell me who I am."

She frowned the small frown that meant she was deciding, then nodded once, quick as a lit match. "Okay."

The white warmed again. The pressure in his hands shifted from held to helped. The stone hummed with a tone he knew not from vents, but from Sunday mornings when a congregation finds itself on the same note without planning.

The other presence retreated a step. Not far. Not defeated. But changed—from predator's curiosity to analyst's interest. We are not finished, it said, wearing his father's voice, which was made of absence. Seals are not sermons. There is blood.

"Faith has blood," he said quietly. "So does love."

The white shivered with something like laughter that never learned manners. Then, like a page being turned, the blank released him.

He was on his knees before the altar, palms pressed to its split. Heat bled through stone into bone. The chapel was a ruin written politely: benches wrenched but not hurled, papers adrift like exhausted birds, the bell still ringing in a tone too pure to be anything but itself.

Ava crouched beside him; wrists red with welted circles. Tears streaked clean through the dust on her cheeks. "Back," she whispered, not a command, an observation. "You came back."

Grayson stood in the doorway, lips moving, hands open—his prayer stripped to essentials: mercy, keep, near. Harker planted herself by the frame, her crushed penlight at her feet, her face equal parts fury and relief. "What did you do," she asked flatly, "and what did it do back?"

"I handed the seam away," Daniel said, voice thin. "I said a name that wasn't its."

Harker filed the answer under later. "We move."

The chapel exhaled, displeased. The altar's wound dimmed, the dark at its base thinning but not gone. They backed out. Daniel's palms burned, but he did not let go until the pressure eased.

The corridor greeted them with the smell of damp stone and faint sweetness of old sanctuaries. Their chalk marks still glowed like nightlights, too small to be logical, too honest to be dismissed.

Back on the ward, chaos had settled into a working mess. Patients huddled under emergency lights. Nurses counted aloud. Ava whispered, "No names. Not theirs."

"I didn't," Daniel said. "Not theirs."

She nodded, half-asleep, shaping Lily's melody without sound.

Harker crouched to meet Daniel's eyes. "You're burned," she said, glancing at his palms. "And you're still you."

"Mostly," he managed.

"Good. Be that, then."

Grayson eased into a chair and murmured, "Sometimes the miracle isn't the lion lying down with the lamb. It's that the ones who stood between them get to stand up again."

Daniel laughed once, brittle and honest. He opened his hands. The prayer stone lay quiet now—whole and broken at once.

In his room, the word still waited on the wall above the sink: FOUR. He smudged one corner with his thumb. No trick. No permanence. Just verdict.

From below, a sound rolled upward—not a boom, but the long, low groan of a vast hinge testing itself.

Daniel gripped the stone. It pressed back—question and answer both.

He did not know if the fifth seal would knock or simply step through. He only knew—in this minute, this breath—that he was not alone.

"Lord," he whispered into the listening, "keep."

The silence held. Not teeth this time. Not yet. And in a world of seams, a single breath can be a door.

Chapter 24: The Fifth Seal

Morning tried.

The emergency lights steadied into a weak, medicinal glow that turned every face a shade too pale. Machines blinked their compliance; a generator droned from somewhere deep, its rhythm like a throat clearing every few seconds. The ward exhaled, but it was the kind of breath you take when you know the room is listening. The silence hadn't left. It had just put on shoes and walked the halls.

Patients clustered in twos and threes. Chairs scraped closer, forming small islands of nervous humanity. A man who hadn't met anyone's eyes in weeks gripped a nurse's hand with the solemnity of a patient signing a do-not-resuscitate. A woman kept her gaze fixed on the window, whispering as if glass could promise her safety. Harker moved among them like a field medic—bandages, calm orders, and a tone that carried invitation instead of command. She spoke as if to wild animals that—for now—had chosen not to bite.

Daniel sat under the light grid, prayer stone turning between his fingers. Whole. Seam. Hairline. Whole again. The burn-ovals on his palms had eased to a warm ache, but the marks beneath his skin—those ribbed circles—still glowed faintly, like embers refusing extinction. He pressed his wrist to the table and felt a pulse that wasn't his own, like a distant bell rung softly, again and again.

At the next table Ava hunched over her sketchbook, pencil carving through paper like rain on stiff leaves. She had stopped pretending the drawings were hers. She didn't ask permission anymore. Her bandaged wrists bled through in small, perfect circles where the marks kept insisting. Under the sickly lights her skin looked thinner, translucent, as though some part of her had surfaced and refused to retreat.

He slid his chair closer. The pages were frantic—scenes, not symbols. Himself, rendered in quick graphite certainty. One drawing showed his shirt clinging as if drenched, his mouth open in a word he didn't want to see written. Another showed him engulfed in flame that looked more like water, clinging rather than consuming. A third split him in two: one Daniel kneeling with open hands, the other standing with fists clenched, the stone between them a thin blade.

Ava didn't look up. Her voice came like someone running to deliver a line before it spoiled.

"It won't be subtle. The fifth. It's going to take more than faith."

Daniel bristled, though he didn't rise. "Faith is not small."

"I didn't say it was." She turned the page hard enough to tear the margin. "I said it won't be enough alone. It will take surrender."

The word struck like a nerve test. He wanted to spit something clever, but no wit came. No saliva, either. Only Lily's voice echoed—seven years old, fifteen years old, both at once—telling him what was his to fix and what wasn't. You can forgive it.

"Then show me how," he said, more plea than argument.

Ava tapped the next sketch: Daniel's open hands, the stone laid across them like an offering. Flames rose, but not the consuming kind—the priestly kind, blessed into meaning.

"You stop asking the dark for answers," she whispered. "You stop carrying the light like a weapon. You hold it like a gift."

He dropped his eyes. Eye contact would have made him lie.

The generator's drone shifted pitch. Somewhere a drip found metal and set a rhythm. Grim normalcy plodded on.

Father Grayson arrived with coffee that tasted like old bells. He set a cup before Daniel and another by Ava's elbow. His hands trembled now, and he refused to explain it.

"I'm opening the chapel in an hour," he said softly. Then, clearer, for their ears alone: "The one upstairs. For prayer."

Ava's mouth twitched. "We'll be in another chapel."

Grayson didn't argue. He only looked at her wrists, winced, and turned to Daniel. Something passed between them—recognition, maybe resignation.

"Surrender isn't the absence of action," he said. "It's the presence of trust."

Before Daniel could answer, Harker appeared with a rolling cart that had stopped pretending to belong to medicine. On it: headlamps, chemical glow sticks, radios, a coil of nylon rope, a first-aid kit rubbed half blank, and a pry bar that looked like it had ended arguments. Heavy gloves folded on top like a quiet benediction.

"If you're going," she said flatly, "go like people who intend to come back."

"We are," Daniel said.

"I am not reassured," she replied, dry. Then, quieter: "But we plan anyway."

She divided the gear with practiced efficiency. Ava and Daniel took headlamps. Grayson got the rope. Harker kept the pry bar. Glow sticks bloomed green in Daniel's palm. The radios coughed static like someone holding breath on the other end.

"Rules," Harker said. "We stay in sight. We mark and count. We keep the door open. If we can't manage two of the three, we return."

"And if the door closes?" Grayson asked.

Harker lifted the pry bar an inch. "Then the door opens."

Ava tore out her final page and handed it to Daniel. Flame. Water. Open hands. The stone bridging both.

"That's your only map," she said.

He slid it behind the stone in his pocket. Reflex made his fingers seek his wedding ring, only to find absence. "Emily," he whispered without meaning to. The name cut the air like a wound that didn't bleed.

The STAFF ONLY door received them like an elevator stopping on the wrong floor. The ward pretended not to watch. A woman crossed herself, then folded her hands together because habit and hope share the same posture. Harker swiped her card. The lock clicked, green.

The stairwell swallowed them with its stretched cold, a blanket thinned too far. Their headlamps carved cones in the dust; Daniel's glow stick trailed a green comet of his hand. Their footfalls fell heavy, echo-less.

They passed the reliquary door. Silent now. They passed the cage with their urgent drag marks. Charcoal hash-marks on the wall looked small and childish against the dark. With each one, the stone in Daniel's pocket pulsed, approving.

The chapel door stood shut, carved with circles deep enough to hold shadow. The seam sealed, exhaling cold through its grooves. Sleeping. Dreaming. They did not enter. Not yet.

Harker pressed a radio into Grayson's hands. "One channel. Don't lose it."

Grayson nodded. To Daniel: "You do not give your mouth."

"I'll try," Daniel said. The truth in his tone carried more weight than the words.

Ava drew her circle-cross on the wall with charcoal, then pressed her bandaged palm against it. She hissed through her teeth. "There. They hate that."

Daniel raised the stone. "Then we keep doing what they hate."

They moved on. The corridor took liberties—angles where there hadn't been angles, stair flights in illogical increments, landings arriving too soon. Pipes sweated. Doors forgot their numbers. Twice Harker shouldered them open. Twice Daniel watched the glow stick light reveal concrete that seemed to remember being stone.

Air thickened. Humidity grew. The smell shifted to riverbed: water, iron, basement mildew. The stone seared his palm in a way that wasn't pain—more like instruction.

"There," Ava whispered.

The corridor narrowed to damp stairs. Harker tossed a glow stick; it bounced, rolled, and came to rest like a faithful insect. The rail was slick, cold. They gripped anyway.

Walls closed inward, ribs around a suffocating lung. The generator faded to rumor. Even the radios seemed shy. Their breathing was the only rhythm left.

At the bottom the hall widened. Their headlamps reached a far wall, then returned. Symbols carved at knee height lined the base, circles softened by time but still whispering. Someone had rubbed them with ash once. The residue clung. Ava brushed a fingertip and gasped—not at heat, but memory.

"Older," she breathed. "Older than the chapel."

To the right, an opening yawned—rough stone, not concrete. Damp walls, earth-scent, air tinged with something alive that had never known light. Daniel raised the stone; its glow grew denser, refusing distance.

"This is where maps come to die," Harker said, awe dressed as report.

Grayson's radio cracked: a nurse's voice, thin with static. "—Father? You copy?—"

"I copy," he said. "We're below. Hold fast. Pray."

"Always." The radio hushed again.

They stood at the threshold. Daniel felt it—the line, the invitation, the pull of terrible mercy. Ava's sketch. Lily's white room. The choice.

Harker met his gaze. He nodded.

They stepped inside.

The walls pressed close, sweating constellations of moisture. The floor shifted from smooth to patterned, stone laid like scales. The marks under Daniel's skin sang low, unignorable. The air reeked of storm cellars and memory.

Then the space opened.

Their lights swung into a chamber vast enough to swallow a chapel, vast enough to echo with its own pulse. A dome rose above, symbols carved in sweeping bands, edges worn soft by centuries. The floor stretched as one slab of stone, interrupted only by a single, immense seam—a fault line the size of a road.

And beneath it, something moved.

Not form. Light. Ancient not-light, older than the chapel's altar, glowing as though the earth itself remembered it had a heart. The seam breathed. Daniel felt it in his knees.

He stepped forward before his mind caught up. The stone in his hand scorched. Ava gripped his sleeve. Harker caught his elbow. Grayson steadied his back.

"Easy," Harker murmured.

"Boundaries," Grayson warned.

"Hold it like a gift," Ava whispered.

Daniel knelt at the seam. Two fingers touched the floor as if testing a sleeping child's fever.

His vision blew open.

Rain on canvas. Emily's braid soaked dark. Lily's hand slipping away again and again. The faceless watcher at the tree. Forest layered over hospital like tracing paper. The chamber beating once, then again, the seam expanding like a lung.

The stone hummed—a tone that remembered pews and mercy and survival. He looked down. The seam widened by a hair. A dim white truth bled upward.

"The fifth," Ava said. Not warning. Naming.

The air thickened. The hush sharpened into teeth.

Daniel closed his eyes. Yours. Pain flared, marks molten to his elbows, then stilled, waiting.

He opened his hands.

He did not offer. He released. Like a breath. Like a grudge. Like a question you cannot keep. The stone lay across his palms like a bridge. For one impossible, ordinary second, he wanted to stop wanting.

The seam inhaled.

The chamber spoke without sound.

And a crack—metal scream and earth-song—wrote itself down the middle of the world.

Chapter 25: The Breach

The crack wrote itself down the world like a sentence no one had consented to read.

Stone shuddered under Daniel's knees. The seam inhaled again—slow, tidal—and every wall in the chamber seemed to lean, then correct, like a tired animal shifting its weight. Headlamps threw their cones and the cones came back wrong, elongated and late. The glow stick's honest green stuttered, then kept faith.

"The pull," Harker said, voice clipped to shape fear into orders. "Stay low. Hands on each other."

Ava's fingers found Daniel's sleeve and stayed, hot through the fabric, the bandages at her wrists bright as flags in the headlamp light. Grayson's palm pressed between Daniel's shoulder blades, a human brace. The rope tugged once at Daniel's waist—Harker's knot holding, a reminder and a promise both.

Time slipped. First by a second, then by a breath. Daniel felt his inhale finish and the room not quite agree. The generator's thrum from far above came late, then early, then right on time, then vanished entirely as if embarrassed to have been overheard down here. Their footfalls landed and then arrived. The edges of the chamber blurred and sharpened, the curve of the dome breathing, widening, narrowing, refusing to accept a single measurement.

Gravity grew ideas. The floor tipped a degree to the left; his stomach noticed before his eyes did. The seam widened by the width of a thumbnail. Dust sifted up instead of down, then thought better of the trick and fell.

Whispers braided the air—not around them, not over them—through them. Emily's laugh, low and tired from a kitchen at midnight, braided with Lily's high clear Daddy and a boy's voice Daniel hadn't heard in years, the one he'd used to ask caseworkers whether this house was the last house. Each syllable carried a hook and a comfort. Each knew where to land.

"Don't answer," Ava breathed, as if reading the muscles in his throat.

"I won't," he said, and believed himself in that moment the way a man believes a rope he tied with his own hands.

They moved to the seam's edge. The floor was one sheet of stone but felt layered, as if something thin and alive lay between surfaces. Symbols ran the inner curve of the dome in bands—a long procession of circles, crosses, bars, hash marks—carved so long ago the tools that cut them might as well have been words. The not-light under the seam surged and sank to its own heartbeat, a radiance so old it had given up on brightness and decided to be true instead.

Daniel set his palm to the floor to steady himself.

The visions didn't arrive; they opened, like the seam—no shock, no flare. The chamber filled his eyes and then stood aside and the forest stepped in, not as memory, not as dream—as angle. Rain stitched the air—fine needles, falling straight until gravity hiccupped and set them slant. The tent's fly flapped, and the sound hung for a second before agreeing to be noise. Emily's braid was damp with patience. Lily's hand was in his, small and warm and entirely present—

—and then not. Not a slip. Not a miss. A taking. The gap between the fingers in his hand and the fingers he was holding widened without space to widen into, and he saw it from outside himself, as if a lens had been mounted in the air. The circle didn't just glow; it registered—like an instrument finding a signal. Something stood at the edge of the clearing, not faceless because it had no face, but because the idea of face was insufficient. A tilt, a listening. The same attention he'd felt in the white, angled toward his life.

He watched himself lunge and fail. He watched Emily's mouth shape his name with a stiffness that meant she understood what could not be undone. He watched the air ripple as the seam below his knees had rippled now, a long, patient split disclosed in light, not line, as if the ground had been pre-broken, waiting for want to pry it open.

The pull below him strengthened. The chamber was very much itself again—wet mineral smell, old heat, tick of water somewhere finding freedom. His palm tingled where it met stone, the tingling sliding up his wrist to meet the marks that had been singing there since the first night.

"Daniel." Grayson's voice sat close, steady. "With us."

"I'm here," he said, and the words went through two rooms to find his mouth.

The seems glow brightened a shade, not enough to light faces—enough to warn nerves. The floor vibrated, a fine, metallic tremor that reminded him of tuning forks and scalpels. Somewhere distant but not far, something metal protested, and the protest reached them late and braided into the hum the room denied it had.

Ava made a sound he had not heard from her before—not pain, not surprise. Awe that hurt. "It's waking in layers," she said. "Like it forgot how and just remembered."

Harker shifted her grip on the pry bar. "We keep the door in sight," she said, and the one rule she could keep did its job of keeping her.

The whispers turned crueler. The boy-Daniel mocked with a perfect imitation of his own defensiveness. Emily's voice took on a softness he knew, the softness that preceded a hard truth. Lily's laughter cracked like thin ice and sank. The chamber answered all of it with the patient indifference of a tide.

The floor drew a breath, and the seam widened enough to become a thing a person could trip on. Heat brushed his palm—exhale from a throat. The old not-light leaked up along the edges, gathering in a fine white line in the crack's shadow. The symbols along the dome brightened a fraction— a pulse, then stillness—as if something large had blinked.

He set both hands down this time, not to claim, not to force—to keep from falling. The stone lay across his fingers like a bright weight. He lifted his face and saw it again—the clearing, the circle, the tilt of attention at the edge. Not an intruder. A witness with appetite.

He understood something he did not want: that he had fed this watcher with why for years, solid meals of focus, midnight snacks of doubt, banquets of imagined control. The thing did not cause the breach. It used it. It wasn't creator, it was carrion with a crown. And he had set a table.

Shame rose fast, efficient, hot. He let it. Then he let it go— the way he had let breath go, the way he had let questions go in the white. "Not yours," he said aloud, not angrily, not bravely. A cashier closing a till. "Not anymore."

The chamber's not-light leaned in. The seam widened another hair.

Ava gasped, both hands snapping to her bandaged wrists. The gauze went bright as snow, then transparent at the seams as the marks beneath burned through with a clean, pitiless white. "They're writing," she choked, and the pencil that had always been there suddenly wasn't. Her fingers curled against the pain and reflex, and Daniel forced himself not to grab her, not to tear the wrappings free. Harker was already there, gentle with hands that had learned gentleness in the oldest classrooms: ERs and funerals and midnight conversations in bad chairs.

Grayson dropped to both knees. He had prayed in this place with dignity and patience and craft; now his prayer tore from somewhere farther back. "Mercy," he said, and then again, and then he couldn't speak for a heartbeat because tears had found his throat. He bent his head to the stone and left it there, a man making himself small to ask for a larger kindness.

The whispering shifted key.

It became metal.

A single, long scream sounded from the far side of the chamber, then from below, then from inside the seam under Daniel's hands, as if the floor were a blade being pulled too fast over an edge. The sound brought its own pressure, shoving at his shoulders and cheeks, making his teeth vibrate in their beds. The dome overhead boomed back once like a drum answering a call. Dust cascaded from the carved bands in a soft, ruthless snow.

"The fifth," Ava said through her teeth, voice gray with pain. "It's breaking. It's—"

The seam yawned.

Not open—apart. Two planes discovering they had always been two and regretting the lie of one. The not-light surged and did not brighten—its truth grew, thickening the air until their headlamps seemed vulgar and unnecessary, cheap flashbulbs at a coronation. The rope at Daniel's waist tugged once—Harker pulling them backward—and for a breath his body argued with physics about where it belonged.

"I've got you," Harker said through clenched teeth. "Back." Her boots found purchase on stone that did not entirely agree it was ground. She dug the pry bar's flattened tongue into a hairline in the floor like a woman levering open a casket she refused to let seal.

The scream of metal grew teeth, then began to shred itself. The symbols on the dome banded with light—one pulse, two—timed to the seam's insistence. The crack bent toward them by a fraction, like a line of handwriting leaning hard later in the sentence.

"Daniel," Grayson said, and he wasn't asking for anything specific—just permission to stand between a man and his breaking. He did it with his body anyway, angling his shoulder so that if the floor made a worse decision, he would be the first thing to meet it.

For a second the whole chamber lagged. Like time. Like breath. Like a heart that has decided whether to keep.

The fifth seal tore.

Not a neat sound, not a single event. A series of rips nested inside a larger one, like a zipper forced too fast, like ice across a lake deciding to be water again all at once. The floor juddered; the dome answered with a heavy thump; a slab shivered under Daniel's knee and then remembered itself at the last possible moment. A wind rose from the seam—not air, exactly. Pressure fleeing. It hit them with a smell like riverbed and old iron and a sweetness that might have been incense burned in a church that had long since stopped believing in smoke alarms.

Ava went down to one elbow and curled around her wrists. The bandages smoldered, edges darkening as if from an unseen flame. She wept without theatrics, breath hitching, cheeks wet. Harker tore the gauze with her teeth, fingers quick and, when the worst had passed, tender. The marks beneath blazed white-hot for three breaths, then faded to a deep, dangerous red. The skin around them had risen in perfect ridges. The symbols were not painted on her; they lived there now, structures in flesh.

Grayson's prayer fell apart. He kept speaking anyway, syllables stumbling into one another, the words no longer pristine petitions but the garbled gratitude of a man who has not been allowed to fall through a floor. Tears lifted the gravel in his voice and made it human in a way his priesthood had never stopped being. Daniel wanted to add his own words and found the best of them had been stolen by awe. He settled for honesty.

"Yours," he whispered into the glow, and the glow did not answer and did not need to.

The seam slowed. The tearing finished its sentence and sat back, satisfied or exhausted. The not-light pooled at the edges, thin as breath. The floor remained two and pretended at one out of courtesy. The dome's carved bands stopped pulsing and went back to their old sleep, merely bright enough to make night work for a living.

The chamber's whispers did not leave. They changed tenor, moving from invitation to assessment. The tilt of attention—that angle he had come to recognize even without a face—reoriented. Not closer. More precise.

He lifted his hands from the floor and found his fingers shaking hard enough to steal the fine work from them. The stone lay across his palms, cool again, seam hair-thin and polite. A small, dark smear of dust had settled into the crease of one lifeline, like punctuation.

"We're done here," Harker said, not pretending it was a suggestion. She got under Ava's arm and lifted with the quiet strength of a person who has moved people who did not want to move. "Back. Now. Before the room changes its mind."

Grayson stood with the help of the pry bar and, after a breath's argument with his knees, kept his feet. He placed a hand between Daniel's shoulders again, not to shove—just to say with you one more time. Daniel got his boots under him, let the rope tug them into a single unit, and took the first step away from the seam.

The chamber watched them go. He could feel it the way one feels the last glance at a party—the look you get when you've said no to something and it has decided to wait for a better answer. The whispers thinned to a braid, then to a thread, then to the frictionless silence of deep stone.

They reached the passage mouth and the air changed to honest damp. The headlamps found the beads of moisture on the wall and made them stars again. The floor became floor. Gravity remembered its manners. The rope around Daniel's waist felt like a hand that had never asked for anything it wouldn't return.

At the first landing, the radios cleared their throats. "—copy?—" came a nurse's voice, thin with distance and relief balanced on terror.

"Copy," Grayson said, and the word released something he hadn't noticed he'd been holding between his teeth.

They climbed. The glow stick on the stairs had bled out most of its green, loyal to the last. At the chapel door, Harker paused, listening with her whole body. The room on the other side kept its own counsel. She opened anyway, pry bar ready, chin up.

They entered the known wrong. The symbols on the chapel walls were dim, the altar seam a scar rather than a wound. The reliquary bell did not ring. It waited.

Ava slumped into the back pew and let her head fall into her hands. Harker checked her wrists and swore softly, professionally, at the burn pattern. Grayson stood in the short aisle and finished the prayer he'd started with tears in it, which is to say he began again.

And Daniel—Daniel stood under the curve of stone and tried to decide what had changed. The answer was not in the walls. It was in him, and it was not large enough to boast and not small enough to hide. The fifth had torn. He had watched the world admit a seam it had been lying about. And he had not fallen through.

He looked down at his palms. The oval burns from the stone had faded to a quiet pink, like the skin around a wedding band after you finally take it off. The marks under his skin had cooled, a deep ember-glow, not demanding, not retreating. Waiting.

He breathed, and the breath did not stumble.

"Back to the ward," Harker said. "We don't linger and we don't celebrate. We count."

They went. The stairwell accepted them, and then the green hallway, and then the swipe of Harker's card and the soothing click of a door that had never been asked to do such heavy symbolic lifting.

On the ward, the generator thrummed its small, brave song. Emergency lights held. Patients turned their heads in unison, eyes flaring with hope or fear, always indistinguishable at first look. A nurse counted them without pretending the numbers were protection, and when the count came out right, she smiled a complicated smile and wrote it down anyway.

Ava sank into her usual chair and pulled a blanket over her knees with a ferocity that said mine. Grayson touched the shoulder of every person who let him. Harker leaned against the glass of the nurses' station, closed her eyes for one breath, then opened them and started giving orders because that was the mercy she knew how to make.

Daniel sat; stone cupped in both hands like a small animal that might stay if he were very kind. The room held. The seam below held. The gap between his wanting and his choosing had not closed—but he had learned its shape.

From somewhere below, too far to rattle the water in the cups and close enough to inform the bones, a low sound rolled and ceased, the way a great door practices between openings.

He did not mistake it for peace. He did not mistake himself for finished.

He whispered anyway, because prayer is not a receipt for outcomes but a surrender to presence.

"Yours."

The word did not answer. It settled. And in a hospital that had learned to live with seams, that was enough to keep the next breath.

Chapter 26: The Spiral

The hospital pretended to hold, but Daniel felt the seams widening again. At first, the ward looked almost normal. Emergency lights glowed their weak yellow, nurses moved through their routines, patients muttered in half-sleep. Then the building shifted. Walls elongated, contracting like lungs. Doors multiplied—some opening to the same room again, others to stairwells that ended against blank walls. Shadows stretched, then lagged behind their owners, sometimes staying after their bodies had gone.

A scream tore down the hall. One patient shouted that another figure was curled into his bed, whispering his name. Another raked her arms bloody, crying that symbols were being written into her flesh. Nurses shouted over the din, voices brittle with panic. Some staff clung to charts and vitals like lifeboats. Others folded their hands and whispered prayers into the electric silence. Order splintered into factions—procedure versus surrender, reason versus reverence—each side accusing the other of making the thing worse.

Daniel pressed his palms to the table, but the whispers came through anyway. They wore Emily's voice, soft and weary from midnight kitchens. They wore Lily's laugh, sharp and bright. They wore his own voice, young and afraid, asking caseworkers if this house would be the last. He almost answered. Almost said Emily. Ava's hand clamped around his wrist before the word escaped, her nails biting into his skin. "That's not her," she hissed. "They only wear her skin." The words stopped him like a slap.

The ache did not stop. Lily flickered in reflections— sometimes a child, sometimes a teenager, sometimes wrong, her eyes black wells that knew his name. Each time she shaped Daddy, his mouth shaped the beginning of a reply. He bit it down until copper rose under his tongue. He wondered whether his presence was unraveling the hospital faster, whether the marks under his skin were prying seams with every beat.

Ava's pencil raced as though dragged by unseen hands. Her sketchbook filled with spirals swallowing corridors, wings, patients, staff. Every spiral led to one figure: Daniel at the center, arms stretched, symbols burned into his flesh, the fire looking like water, the water like flame. She shoved a page at him, voice shaking. "They're pulling you. You're the doorway. If you fall, we all fall."

Grayson fought the collapse with prayer. He gathered chairs in a circle and coaxed staff and patients into it, his voice low and steady: Lord, keep us. Lord, near. Mercy, mercy. For a time, it worked. Panic softened. Even Harker stood nearby, arms folded but listening. When he ended, his lips kept moving, silent, tears stinging his eyes. Daniel caught the whisper: "Silence is not absence. It's waiting."

Harker clung to the language of medicine, resetting charts, barking orders, treating procedure like a weapon. The ward snapped at her and obeyed because routine is a kind of mercy. That night she pulled Daniel aside, voice shaking. "It's on my wall. Ash. One word. FIVE." She didn't explain it away. She rubbed her temple and said, bare: "Pray for me." She couldn't bow her head, but asking was surrender enough.

The hospital screamed. Alarms shrieked though no power fed them. Patients convulsed, chanting in languages they'd never spoken. A pane of reinforced glass bowed inward as if something pressed against it from the other side. Symbols seared across the ceiling, glowing faint as dying stars. Nurses cried out, patients clawed their faces, and over it all the silence pressed like a hand smothering the room.

Daniel folded against the wall. His marks flared molten, dragging his arms down like anchors. Emily breathed at his ear—Come home, Dan. You've worked hard enough. The first letter of her name rose to his teeth. "Em—"

Ava's fingers dug crescent moons into his forearm. "That's the cost," she said, panting. "They want your mouth."

He closed it until jaw pain made his eyes water.

She ripped another page from her sketchbook and shoved it into his hands. A stairwell spiraled down into black, the lines jagged and desperate. "There's more," she rasped. "Below the chamber. Below everything we've seen."

The pull was relentless. Daniel felt his lips move before he heard the words, soft and certain, sealing the chapter like a prayer and a curse all at once.

"The sixth is calling."

Chapter 27: The Sixth Seal

The stairwell didn't so much descend as unwind. Each flight proposed a rule and canceled it on the next. Steps lengthened into gray miles that burned calves and boiled breath—and then, without transition, shrank to jittering inches, forcing them to half-hop, half-crawl like children pretending at giants. The handrail wept a slick, black condensation that swelled and shrank with a pulse Daniel could feel but not hear. When his fingers brushed it, the wet left his skin colder than metal and greasier than grief.

Headlamps threw cones that bent midair, light deciding it had opinions. The glow sticks in Harker's pocket shone through fabric in steady curves—then, for three breaths, arced the wrong way, light bowing to a gravity that tested possibilities. Radios ticked in their hands with a faint digital metronome that measured seconds backward, then forward, as if time were learning to two-step.

Daniel glanced down and saw his own fingers momentarily skeletal, tendons high like harp strings. He jerked and looked away just as Ava's profile went blank—features washed smooth as chalk in rain. He blinked hard. Harker's knuckles flashed older by decades and then young again, skin tightening and loosening as if a sped season rippled beneath. Father Grayson's hand on the rope at Daniel's waist was the only reliable thing—brown, blunt, work-true—as he muttered through teeth set to prayer: "Lord—near. Lord—keep."

The whispers arrived like weather, no doorway, no knock. Emily: Come home, Dan. It's late. You've worked hard enough. Lily: You let me go. A boy's voice from a thin-linoleum kitchen: You were never enough, and God was never enough for you. The braid of them tightened into a rope around Daniel's throat and tugged—down, always down.

Ava tried to draw herself a door. She wedged the sketchbook against her thigh and scribbled mid-step; the paper browned at the center, crisped to black in a widening ring, and floated apart as ash before the graphite finished its thought. She hissed and tore out the next page. This time the pencil burned a white line as if the paper were a negative of light. She dropped the book and clamped her wrists to her ribs. The bandages there had already blotted—skin beneath the gauze writing without her, the red circles raising like hot coins.

Halfway, Harker stopped. Not a stumble. A refusal. She braced one palm to the sweating wall, penlight swinging mad arcs, listening with her whole face. "I hear her," she whispered, and the word her had edges. "My daughter— she—she needs me." The rest broke apart in her mouth.

Daniel caught her elbow before listening became falling. "No," he said, louder than he meant. "She's alive. She's home. That voice isn't hers. It's what's using yours." Harker's jaw trembled, grief making a brief, indecent show in the set of her mouth. Grayson slid beside them and wrapped his fingers around her wrist—not yanking, not soothing, anchoring. "Do not let them spend your love for their hunger," he said. Harker nodded once—like a soldier at the sound of her own name—and kept moving.

The stairwell opened. Ground forgot how to be floor and remembered how to be chamber. Their lamps hit a space so large the light gave up at the edges, lay down, and panted. The walls spiraled with a geometry that mocked maps. Bands of symbols crawled as if insects had chosen pilgrimage and the stone had obliged by becoming writable. Corners curved. The dome above breathed with them—long inhale that raised the ceiling a fraction; long exhale that dropped dust; a subsonic hum that rattled teeth and set a dry ache at the bridge of the nose. Iron touched his tongue. His ears counted a second heartbeat and tried to forget how.

In the center waited the chasm: the first darkness he had met that glowed. Not-light pooled there, black so dense it poured, like tar with its own radiance. The edges pulsed in, out, in, like a sleeping thing deciding whether to wake. Breath rose out of it—rot thinned with something sweet enough to be incense if you didn't know better; mid-notes of old metal and riverbed and sun-warmed sandstone that had never seen this far down.

Then the cavern filled with awareness.

It didn't arrive; it allowed their noticing. Like discovering the house you've lived in forever has a second story. Presence pressed outward from the chasm and soaked the stone until every surface was intention. Faces flickered at the periphery—cheeks and jaws and eyes that belonged to no one and everyone—limbs elongated wrong, Daniel's own profile stretched in the reflective slick of wall, grin miscalculated. The awareness tried on voices like coats in a mirror: Emily's low laugh; Lily's delighted shriek at a jump rope finally mastered; Grayson's prayer pitch-shifted mean; Daniel's lecture cadence thinned and smug.

It showed a kitchen unruined by absence. Flour dust in sun. A red bowl. Emily in her old sweater, braid over shoulder, smoothing dough with the palm-flat motion he loved because it meant tomorrow existed. Lily's small hands powdered white, puffing a cloud at him, laughing when he pretended to choke. The sound that left him wasn't speech. The Breaker (he would not name it as a name) layered a whisper into the warmth: Faith is silence, Daniel. You asked for answers. I will give you all the answers. No more why. No more hunger. Only stillness and promise kept.

He stepped before knowing he had moved. The rope at his waist tugged; Grayson's hand set a firm square between his shoulders. Emily's eyes were whole, not abyssal; her smile had that old half-crooked for jokes that almost landed and were loved for trying. His mouth shaped the syllables he had sworn not to give—two letters, then four, then the vowel that turns a throat into a cradle.

The stone burned like a careful brand. Pain shot up his wrists, into the thin ribbed circles under his skin. Each mark caught heat and sang it back like strings plucked by a surgeon.

Ava's scream sheared the kitchen in half. She slammed into him with the strength that lives in bodies that weigh less than fear, fingers dragging red crescents down his sleeves. "Don't carry it like a weapon," she shouted in his face, tears and graphite and dust on her mouth. "Hold it like a gift." She dropped to her knees and clawed at the cavern floor, etching a circle and bar and cross, smearing the lines with blood where her cuticles tore. Primitive, childish marks—and the room recoiled anyway, the way heat recoils from certain metals.

Grayson's voice jumped from liturgy to roar. "Lord be near. Lord keep." Not careful now—this was a man throwing his body across a threshold, blessing and forbidding in the same breath. The third repetition cracked his voice; he kept going because some words stay true even when their delivery breaks.

Emily sagged at the edges like wax under heat. Lily's hands blurred. The red bowl collapsed like paper in rain. The presence laughed, the sound dropping through octaves until dust hopped and Daniel's bones rang like little bells. He didn't look at it. He let the stone choose his gaze. He did not raise it like a blade. He opened both palms and let it rest there—a bridge, not a knife.

The chamber convulsed. The chasm tore itself wider with a sound like a ship's hull scraping reef, like every old hospital door's handle being wrenched off at once. Light—no, truth—pushed up the edges in a fine white seam. The bands of symbols along the spiraled walls flared with a workman's brightness—no theatrical blaze; a hard utility—and split along hairlines so ancient the rock must have been born with them. Fragments sheared into the air, sharp as glass and small as flour, filling their beams with a snow of knives.

Ava folded; wind knocked out of a small bird. The gauze at her wrists smoked, edges furling like scorched lace. Blood ran not in gushes but in thin, sure lines, precise as ink. Harker ripped the wrappings with her teeth and swore, hands already steri-stripping what could be pulled together, pressing gauze that would scald as it stuck, whispering nonsense comfort because the body believes quiet nonsense better than shouted truth. "Breathe. Breathe." Ava breathed and cried without sound and pressed her wrists into Harker's hands with a trust neither had earned and both deserved.

Grayson staggered and caught himself on the pry bar like a man leaning into high wind. He shut his eyes, opened them with the fury of someone choosing presence at cost. "Mercy," he said, then, bargaining with oceans, "not for outcome, Lord—for nearness."

Harker's composure—so carefully stapled—gave. "This isn't possible," she said into the roar. Louder: "This isn't possible." Then, naked: "I don't know what to do." The admission cut a new kind of space in the room—thinner, more breathable than air had been.

The rope at Daniel's waist pulled him one inch backward— Harker's silent insistence that bodies stay countable. He planted his feet at the lip. The stone had become a small star, not blinding—indomitable. Courage radiated from it in a way that made his seem counterfeit unless aligned. The marks under his skin flared and dimmed to its rhythm, a communion of scars and light.

The presence tried one last kindness that wasn't. Say my name, it breathed—effortless, intimate as a friend's fingers braiding your hair. Names are doors. Your mouth has drawn me for years. Let me sit in it. I'll sing your lost into the room. You'll never ask why again. You'll never have to pray into silence.

He had learned something in the white that words couldn't improve. He answered without eloquence. "No." Then, to tell the truth while telling it to the dark: "I want to. But no."

The chasm shuddered like a beast denied promised meat. The scream of metal rose, frayed. The dome thumped back, heavy, shaking veils of dust from carved bands. The floor rolled a small warning under his boots, like an elementary earthquake drill practicing for a big wrong.

He closed his eyes and stayed. "Jesus," he said—not as warding, not as spell, as address to a hand large enough to take the seam. "Yours."

The sensation wasn't triumph. It was weight shifting from his hands to stronger ones. Pressure pressing down that read helped rather than held. A bell very far off rang three precise notes—the reliquary upstairs would have remembered them if brass kept memories.

The cavern decided.

With a series of nested rips—a zipper forced and forced again—the sixth tore. The chasm's edge found a new position and sat there, wider by the width of a truth. Not-light rose, pooled higher for a breath, then flattened the way a last tide lick resigns to hush. The symbols cut their glow like laborers at quitting time—an end to overtime, a promise to return. Shards hung, drifted, and fell without slicing what physics insisted they should, as if the math had become merciful for a minute.

Silence fell hard, exact, ringing with the memory of loud.

Dust hovered like pollen. Headlamps resumed their vulgar modern punctuation in an ancient sentence. The rope at Daniel's waist tugged once, soft. Grayson breathed with effort, but breathed. Harker kept one hand on Ava's shoulder and one on the gauze, making a small, stubborn island of medicine inside a theology she refused to name.

Daniel stood at the lip. The stone cooled to human temperature—trustworthy. His legs shook. His teeth clicked once together, a small animal sound he couldn't help. His face was wet; he didn't remember when.

From below, the not-light breathed—ordinary measures now, as if the abyss had lungs and was willing to be heard again at human scale. The presence didn't leave. It tipped from predator to analyst and waited with the patience of a long game.

"Count," Harker said, voice husked but steady, and the practical mercy of numbers stepped back into the room. "Breaths. People. Steps." She looked at Daniel with eyes washed in something that wasn't science and hadn't drowned her. "Stay with us." Not a command—a blessing shaped like one.

He didn't answer her. The abyss did.

Lily's voice rose from the seam. Not strained. Not pleading. Not borrowed. A fact. Summer-sweet, the way her breath had felt when she fell asleep in the car and he'd carried her upstairs, her cheek warm on his shoulder.

"One left, Daddy," she said. "One more."

The words settled careful as cups on a table. The cavern held its breath the way a congregation does when the last verse ends and no one knows whether they will be asked to speak or be still.

Daniel closed his hands around the stone—not gripping; sheltering. His knees remembered how to lock. The sixth had broken, and the world not ending wasn't proof of smallness; it was the gift of time. The marks under his skin cooled to ember. In the corner of his eye, Grayson bowed his head in thanks that wasn't a victory speech. Harker blinked hard, reset her shoulders like someone choosing usefulness after being undone. Ava leaned her forehead to the cold floor for two breaths, then sat up, wrists wrapped by hands not her own.

The silence wasn't empty. It felt like a palm just above the hair, not quite touching.

He backed from the lip. The rope gathered slack. Somewhere above, a generator coughed and elected to go on humming. Dust made small constellations in their beams. The stairwell waited, promising wrong geometry as the price of leaving.

"One left," Daniel said under his breath—not echo, agreement. He didn't add I'm afraid. He didn't need to. The stone warmed a fraction, as if a larger palm bracketed it for an instant, and the cavern—alive, listening—waited for the seventh.

Chapter 28: The Seventh Seal

Silence fell like a curtain with weight sewn into the hem.

No scream of stone, no thunder, no complaint from the bulbs—only absence, sudden and exact. Alarms froze open-mouthed. The generator's-tired throat closed. Even the little proofs a room is alive—the skim of a sleeve, the breath-litter human beings shed—vanished as if a great thumb found the world's soft spot and pressed.

Daniel did not hear his own inhale. He felt it: ribs widening, a hinge deciding. The floor steadied under his knees—no longer a lung, no longer a tide—yet the quiet pressed his eardrums like deep water. He turned toward the others and found them by a sight that wasn't exactly eyes: Ava with her mouth moving, syllables chewed and useless; Grayson's hand mid-blessing, palm stranded between air and intent; Harker stiff-backed, a fist tucked to her sternum as if a wire had been plucked there. He could see them and could not reach them. Something transparent and heavy hung between them, thin as breath, thick as leaded glass.

He was alone.

The chapel elongated as if distance remembered it could lie. Walls climbed into an unfinished sky. The baseboard's red pulse—gone. The bulbs flickered in a rhythm more like dying than like light. Tile stretched into the kind of long that makes ankles imagine forever. Only the warmth in his hands anchored him: the prayer stone, no longer fierce, simply steady, a small hearth cupped between two human pages.

"Daddy."

Lily's voice. Clear, close, threaded with summer-sweet from back seats and sunburnt naps.

"This is the last," she said. "Are you ready?"

The question knew where to look. He closed his eyes, and a sob that made no sound rose and broke and made him dizzy with how large soundless things can be. When he opened them, the room had acquired its center.

The Breaker did not arrive with spectacle. No beast, no roar. It took a posture in the space between his want and his God and wore intimacy like a suit cut to his measure. Attention tipped toward him—familiar as a friend leaning in, terrible as a cliff's lip.

It spoke, and each syllable entered the stillness like ink into milk, curling wider than seemed possible.

"I can give you peace," it said, and peace meant kitchen. Peace meant the red mixing bowl and flour on the counter and the sound a wooden spoon makes against ceramic. It meant Emily's old sweater, the sleeve slipping to her wrist as she brushed hair from her forehead with the back of her hand. It meant her warmth at his arm, that domestic heat that is not fire and therefore lasts. "You don't have to ache anymore. You don't have to drown in questions. Stay here. Stay with the answer."

The silence accepted the picture and made room for it. Emily turned and gave him the crooked almost-smile that forgave his worst jokes for trying. Lily leaned her small shoulder into his knee and looked up, eyes too alive to be trick light. He could smell cheap coffee and cinnamon and rain ghosting from a jacket hung to dry.

"You prayed," the presence murmured, the cadence an affectionate theft. "Heaven was silent. I answer. I am presence. I am voice. Speak my name, Daniel, and the ache ends."

He wanted to. Not from despair. From love so honest it made defense look like a sin. The old ache opened like a door and his whole life stepped through it: the boy who waited for engines; the man who indexed the world into a safety he could shelve; the father who had reached and missed and had been reaching ever since. His lips trembled toward shape. The mouth remembers its prayers and its betrayals. It knows the weight of names.

L— he thought, and the consonant formed like a ledge.

The stone warmed; it did not burn. Its heat found the thin, ribbed circles under his skin and tuned them like strings a careful hand had kept for a better song. The warmth steadied nothing. It steadied him. He kept looking at the picture because not looking at love is not a courage he respects.

Ava's warning lived at the back of his teeth like a splinter he refused to pull. Don't speak to them. Don't let them in. Grayson's quiet insistence braided under it. Prayer is the light you carry when the door opens. And Emily—not this flour-and-sweater Emily, but the one who had stood in a dark kitchen and rested her head against the cabinet because bills came like tides—We can't know everything's why, Dan. We can know what love does.

The Breaker felt the tremor and made kindness of it. The warmth of Emily's hand moved along his knuckles. Not picture—weight. The floor under him learned their kitchen's pattern and the chapel took that instruction without argument. Lily's laugh rose with the exact ghost of the lisp she'd carried for six weeks at five. She breathed against his wrist and the little hairs there remembered how to lift when a child's exhale finds them.

His mouth opened. The forbidden syllables gathered. The name that had fed his midnight leapt like a relieved apology—

He caught the edges of the stone as if catching himself. "I—"

The vowel that makes a throat into a cradle waited at the lip of his tongue. He chose not to shape it. Not because he wasn't starving. Because starving is not the same as being fed.

"If you could give," he said into a silence that took weight from every word, "you wouldn't have to bargain."

Nothing moved because motion had been dismissed, yet intention leaned. Pity gave the picture angles—sharper, nearer. Emily's thumb traced the old, unconscious rhythm along his knuckle. Lily's chin tipped with that familiar decision. He felt the syllables flood back, a pressure behind good hinges.

"Say my name," it breathed. "Names are doors. You have drawn mine with your questions. Let me sit in your voice. I

237

will sing your lost into the room. You will never have to pray into this again."

He had prayed into this and found a Person instead of a plan. The memory rose not as argument, but as presence on its own: a thirteen-year-old boy on a thin mattress in a good-enough house, naming Jesus like a dare and waking to hope like oxygen. The ridiculousness of love in a white room remained the only non-absurd thing he knew.

He knelt. Not to the presence. To the One whose silence had stopped being empty the night it first met him.

"I can't fix it," he said. The confession entered a space that refused echoes because it tasked words with work. "I can't change it. I can forgive it. Because I was forgiven first."

The stone answered without light; the seam inside it found room. A hairline opened—not breaking apart, opening—and something warm as breath and unshowy as mercy moved along his palms. The pressure in his head let go by a shade, like a glove half unsheathed.

The presence twisted, shapes unraveling like paper in rain. It tried on three more faces and each dropped from it like coats off a nail. It swelled to monstrosity and shrank to a thin cleverness. It did not roar; it recalculated. He felt how

238

forgiveness robs appetite—how a predator despises prey that won't act like food.

"Daddy."

Lily stood in the seam between silences—the white he had met before and the ordinary this room had forgotten. She was seven and she was fifteen; Bun-Bun's one stitched eye caught a light that didn't exist. She looked at the stone, then at his face.

"You can't fix it," she said, solemn with the dignity children give truth when it's heavy. "You can forgive it."

He wanted to ask the easy cruelty, Forgive who? He wanted to ask the ache, Are you— He did not. Answers have appetites. He fed a better thing.

"I'm sorry," he said, and meant it past his body's limits. "For needing why more than love. For trying to pry you out of the hand that holds you because I couldn't bear not being that hand. For letting the mark tell me who I am."

She frowned the small offended frown she saved for math done incorrectly and then nodded once, quick as a match deciding.

"Okay."

The word entered the quiet and settled like a small, obedient animal. The pressure on his hands shifted from held to helped, the seam joining under fingers larger than his. Far above them, the reliquary bell—if brass remembered—would have known the tone: not triumph, not fanfare. Three small notes of agreement.

The Breaker stepped back—not distance, precision. The tilt changed from hunter's curiosity to a clinical patience that counts in years. We are not finished, it breathed, wearing only his father's timbre now, which was made of absence. Seals are not sermons. There is blood.

"Faith has blood," he said, and didn't decorate it. "So does love."

The white shivered with laughter that had never learned manners.

Then the world turned the page.

Sound returned like tide: first the lace at the edge, then the long pull. The chapel contracted to its bad geometry and honest materials. Dust fell with gravity again. The altar's split sat like a cauterized wound—no longer gaping, not yet healed. The darker-than-dark coiled at its base thinned to a film that refused to commit to shadow or smoke.

Ava was beside him before he had wholly arrived, wrists swaddled, gauze edges browned from a heat without flame. Tear tracks cut clean lines down the gray on her cheeks. "Back," she whispered—not proud, not incredulous. Naming.

Grayson stood in the doorway as if deputized by the building itself, hands open, lips working the planks of prayer that had outlived seas and surgeons: mercy, near, keep. His voice was ragged with use and still workman-true. Harker rocked on her heels once and came up fast, eyes red and furious, relief ricocheting into orders before it could be thanked.

"What did you do," she said, a physician's sentence without punctuation, "and what did it do back?"

"I handed the seam away," he said, hearing the truth of how small his part had been. "I said a name that wasn't its."

Harker filed it under later and pointed with her whole body at the exit. "We move. Now."

They moved. The chapel breathed, displeased but outvoted. In the corridor, their charcoal marks still held their small courage on the wall. The stairwell received them with its clean-wet smell and gave them back to the ward with a mechanical exhale that let the lights choose a faint hum and keep it.

Upstairs, the hospital remembered how to misbehave instead of how to be monstrous. Nurses counted aloud with exhausted dignity. Patients blinked beneath emergency grids, pencil sketches trying to remember the trick of becoming people. Harker placed three orders that sounded like mercy. Grayson touched shoulders with a hand that had learned its own small sacraments. Ava claimed her usual chair and guarded her bandaged wrists the way you guard a shoreline the sea has examined more than once.

Daniel stood and listened for the hum that had nested in his bones for days. It wasn't there. The silence had not left; it had changed posture. Not absence—attention.

He went to his room because a man is allowed to check his private altars after public storms. Above the sink, the ash letters waited, dull as judgments.

FOUR.

He smudged a corner with his thumb, made the word human again—erasable if not forgotten. The tap ran cold and ordinary, rinsing gray to clear to nothing. In the mirror, his face looked older by a year and younger by an hour. His palms were oval-burned where the stone had rested, the skin unblistered and unwilling to boast.

When he returned to the dayroom, the ward had gathered itself the way a shaken animal settles without trusting the hand that stroked it. Harker spoke at the glass to a security guard who nodded like nodding was policy. Grayson sat down hard and looked grateful for the invention of chairs. Ava slept with her mouth open and a pencil still in her fist because love is a habit.

From below, a sound rose—not a boom, not a crack, but a long, low roll, like a vast door trying its hinges and choosing not to complain the next time it opened.

Daniel closed his fingers around the stone and felt the seam answer his palm—question and reply braided until calling them two seemed like superstition.

He did not know if the seventh would knock or simply step through. He did not know if he would be enough, or faith would be enough, or forgiveness would find hands when the room asked for blood. He knew—in this honest breath that belonged to itself and nothing more—that he was not alone.

"Lord," he said into the not-quiet, into walls and woods stitched through one another, into a silence that was not empty, "keep."

The room kept.

The quiet did not feel like teeth. It felt like a hand held just above the crown, not quite touching—the pause before a song begins. And in a world made of seams, a minute like that is a door.

Epilogue

Morning sunlight streamed through the lecture hall windows at Regent University, laying soft rectangles across the desks. The room was fuller than usual, but quieter too—students leaning forward, pens paused midair, as Daniel Cross paced at the front.

He looked older than the man who had stood there months ago. His shoulders carried gravity that came from more than academic weight, and his voice no longer reached for certainty but for mystery.

"We look for answers," he told them, pausing at the blackboard, chalk balanced between his fingers. "But sometimes the silence we fear most is not absence. It is presence—waiting for us to listen."

Some students scribbled notes; others simply stared, caught by the cadence of someone who had lived his words in fire. Daniel let the chalk rest on the ledge and let the silence linger—not to unsettle, but to teach.

Later, in his office, the towers of books stood differently— less frantic, more deliberate. A small wooden box sat among them. Inside lay the fractured stone, dull and ordinary now, a relic of something beyond comprehension. Daniel set it beside his well-worn Bible and brushed his fingers across both. His prayer was simple, whispered not for answers, but for strength.

Letters came often. Ava's sketches arrived folded into envelopes, the lines no longer burning, now spirals that opened outward instead of folding inward. She was healing, though her scars spoke their own permanent language. Father Grayson wrote less, but each line was steady: Still here. Still praying. Still near. Harker had resigned from the ward, but Daniel had heard she was volunteering at a hospice—sitting quietly with the dying, not speaking of faith but no longer denying its possibility.

At night, Daniel still woke sometimes at 3:07, pulse hammering, the old questions pressing against his ribs. But instead of turning to broken circles and fevered memories, he folded his hands and whispered into the dark. The silence never gave him words, but it met him. That was enough.

On the mantel above his fireplace, photographs of Emily and Lily remained—unchanged, untarnished. Once they had undone him. Now they steadied him. The ache was still there, but softened, tempered by something he could not name without cheapening it.

That evening, Daniel stepped outside. The air was cool, the horizon painted in pale colors. He stood a long while, watching the world breathe, and let the quiet settle.

The fractured stone in his pocket felt warm, though it had not held light for months. He closed his hand around it, lifted his eyes skyward, and smiled through the sting of tears.

"The silence isn't empty," he whispered. "It's waiting."

For the first time in years, Daniel Cross felt the quiet as a gift.

The silence is not absence. It is waiting.

Meet the Author

Elijah Nightwell writes at the crossroads of faith, fear, and the unseen. His stories explore the thin line between reality and the supernatural, weaving suspense, horror, and hope into narratives that keep readers turning pages long into the night.

Drawn to the power of silence, questions, and the mysteries we cannot easily explain, Elijah crafts thrillers that are as much about the human soul as they are about the darkness pressing against it. His influences include classic Christian suspense, modern psychological horror, and timeless Scripture, but his voice is uniquely his own—gritty, gripping, and relentlessly honest.

When he isn't writing, Elijah can often be found reading theology, walking beneath storm-heavy skies, or sketching out the next tale that refuses to let him go. He believes stories matter most when they both unsettle and heal, when they remind us that even in silence, God is not absent.

Sealbreaker is his debut novel, a haunting and redemptive thriller about obsession, loss, and the presence that waits in silence.

www.ingramcontent.com/pod-product-compliance
Lightning Source LLC
Chambersburg PA
CBHW051944220626
47052CB00004B/789